Lie in the Grave

Lie in the Grave

Michael E Koontz

iUniverse, Inc.
New York   Bloomington

Lie in the Grave

This is a work of fiction. All of the characters, names, incidents, organizations, and dialogue in this novel are either the products of the author's imagination or are used fictitiously.

iUniverse books may be ordered through booksellers or by contacting:

iUniverse
1663 Liberty Drive
Bloomington, IN 47403
www.iuniverse.com
1-800-Authors (1-800-288-4677)

Because of the dynamic nature of the Internet, any Web addresses or links contained in this book may have changed since publication and may no longer be valid. The views expressed in this work are solely those of the author and do not necessarily reflect the views of the publisher, and the publisher hereby disclaims any responsibility for them.

ISBN: 978-1-4401-4431-8 (pbk)
ISBN: 978-1-4401-4432-5 (ebk)

Printed in the United States of America

iUniverse rev. date: 6/19/2009

Cover by John Sternig of Perception LLC – www.beperceived.com

DEDICATION

To my grandson Isaiah:
May he read this and be inspired.

SPECIAL THANKS

To Randee for her insight and expertise.

CHAPTER 1

The woods are eerie today. There's damp air coming in from the west, with a stale odor of trouble swirling about. It's kind of like driving down the road after someone hit a skunk. You know what it is; you just haven't found him it. Gray puffy clouds came rolling in fast this morning. The covering is so dense right now, the morning never stood a chance. But no matter, even on the worst of days the beauty of this place cannot be overshadowed or covered up by anything Mother Nature or Old Man Winter throws at it.

It's the first Saturday in October and a special time of the year here in Pennsylvania. It's the season when the forest is overrun with impatient men and women toting bows and arrows and tree stands, and hopes of conquering their nightly visions. It's the first day of bow season. It's a date most hunters had marked on their calendars months in advance, along with their kids' birthdays, an upcoming dentist appointment, and that all-important three thousand mile oil change.

I stop my Jeep on top of Martin's Road where Johnson Trail crosses over. I lean back into my leather seat and stare down into the valley to my right. I ponder why this place is so magical to me. What is it about the forest that intoxicates me, and yet causes fear and anxiety in most others? Why do some of us treasure the isolated beauty as no less than heaven on earth, and others a trap filled with pitfalls and peril at every turn? I don't have the answer; but I do know where I stand.

Each sacred moment out here allows me the time to reflect on life. It's that rare chance to experience Mother Nature in her purest form. Every tree, every bush, every leaf on the ground, every animal above me or at eye level is a reflection of what is good – what is right with this world. Every hunter knows this. It's why we get up at three o'clock in the morning on a perfectly good Autumn Saturday instead of sleeping in like most normal people. It's the reason we travel hours through back roads and brave weather that would shut down most cities. It's what makes us climb elevations only cell towers dare to journey. We do all this for one reason and one reason only; just so we have the opportunity to be part of something special for just one day. I sure hope this secret never gets out.

Brian Morgan shared these same passions. Growing up in a small town just outside Pittsburgh with his two older sisters, hunting was a tradition for the men in his family. And since the only two men were himself and his father, one could only imagine the bond they shared over the years.

Brian's dad was his buddy – his role model. He was a man who always worked two jobs to ensure everyone in his family had whatever they needed and more. Brian can't recall a day when he wasn't there for him. He often wonders how dad was able to pull that off. But his father met his match this past summer. Heartache took the old guy while mowing one hot afternoon.

Brian is now thirty-five years old and has a son of his own. With a few nice bucks already hanging on the wall back at the house, he looks forward to the day he can take his son out and introduce him to this one important aspect of life. The boy just turned five years old last week so he's got a lot of time to plan the big day. It always brings a smile to Brian's face whenever he thinks about it. How great it's going to be the first time his son sees a deer walk up. The excitement he'll feel when he gets his first opportunity to draw down on a nice one. But for now, it's just a dream.

———————

Brian arrives at the base of the mountain around five o'clock, before the sun has a chance to give away his position. He parks his Chevy Silverado in the parking lot on the west side of the mountain, as he does each and every year. He finds himself being the first one here this morning and feels like he has won something. Is there some accomplishment in beating everyone into the woods? In the back of his mind, he knows the answer.

The headlights are killed as the heavy-duty V8 comes to a halt. Brian slowly rolls down his window, leans back into the seat, and listens to the wind as it cuts through the trees that soar above him. Looking off to the east, he takes notice of the clouds that have consumed the lower elevations on the mountain. He hopes the sun can take care of this problem but is not confident about the outcome. Either way, he hunts today.

After a final drag from his cigarette, Brian exits the vehicle and begins the task of retrieving hunting gear from the bed of his truck. Within minutes he has everything he needs for the day suspended onto his back. He bypasses the yellow cast iron gate that separates the parking lot from the woods and begins the three-mile climb up the dirt road to his annual destination.

This year was going to be a different hunt for sure. Something was going to be missing and he knew it before even starting out this morning. This trip would be the first one without dad by his side.

As Brian starts his climb up the mountain, he is consumed with the sadness of this fact. Tears are streaming down his face, as he continues walking up the steep incline. His love for the outdoors is strong and he knows if he doesn't continue the tradition, dad would not be pleased. Besides; his son will be able to hunt in a few years, which immediately brought joy to a much-needed aching heart. Before long, he'll have someone along side to share all the great memories he and his father had created over the years.

It's six o'clock when Brian completes his three-mile hike. With sweat pouring down his brow, he stands looking down Johnson Trail and into the valley that will lead him to his favorite hunting spot. The woods are dark this morning. With a moon unable to penetrate a sky filled with clouds, a man can barely see his hand in front of his face. With the aid of his mini flashlight, Brian finds his handkerchief and wipes his brow dry before heading down the ravine. He didn't use to sweat so much after walking back here. Years and gravity have a tendency to wear on the best of us. He is aware of his mortality and accepts it with dignity.

By six-twenty he arrives at his spot, which is a few hundred yards off the trail. A misty rain fell during the night hours making the bed of leaves that have fallen to earth over the years as quiet as a walk on fresh shag carpet. The weather man said the high temperature today would be around fifty degrees with a light wind coming from the east. And the best news of all - no more rain in the forecast.

Brian gets himself ready for the day by first laying out his equipment in such a way that he can retrieve it fast. One never knows when the need will arise to make a quick shot on a running trophy. His bow is a compound; a 'Martin' no less. Best money can buy. He carefully places it just to his right. He suspends his camouflaged backpack on a close hanging branch to his left. This is where all the good stuff is stored like a thermos full of hot coffee, candy bars, and a few ham sandwiches his wife prepared for him the night before. He doesn't have to check to see what's on them either. He knows. Three slices of ham, mayo, lettuce, and a slice of tomato. Brian's only challenge will be to wait until noon to devour them. He fails every year.

After getting his things in order, Brian grabs a smoke from his left breast pocket and begins digging around for his lighter. That's when he hears it: The snapping of a branch just to his left. He knows from experience that wood of any size doesn't make noise unless pressure is applied.

He slowly turns his head. The sun has yet to crest the mountain so visibility has not improved much. In fact, it's pretty much non-existent down in this sheltered ravine. He strains at the outline of a figure coming toward him in the darkness. It appears to be that of a man but he can't be sure. He reaches for his backpack and attempts to secure his flashlight, but the moist ground has allowed the intruder to get way too close too soon. Brian finds out too late that he is in trouble, and out of time.

Suddenly, he feels a stinging pain on the left side of his neck: A pain much like that of a bee or wasp sting. He reaches for the affected area with his hand and finds something stuck in him. Brian begins to panic. His mind says run but his body won't move. He makes mental plans to get away from the unknown entity, but he cannot carry them out. He yells out in desperation, trying to scare off his pursuer. His efforts are ignored.

Before he can even blink his eyes again, he feels the pressure of the impact on his left side. He reaches for the pain and can feel the warmth – the limited supply of the life-giving blood leaving his body. He leans back against the tree once again. He can now see his pursuer but has no strength to fight back. He has no energy to take on the beast that just killed him. All Brian wanted to do is spend a relaxing day in the woods. Sometimes you have to be careful what you wish for.

CHAPTER 2

Death is just...creepy. It's not something the average person looks forward to staring at or being around for any length of time. And I'm not talking about someone dying of old age or natural causes. Those folks are the lucky ones. They have a chance to digest death and at least exit this world with some dignity. Staring at a human being who has died peacefully is somewhat surreal. It kind of reminds you of someone taking a nap on the couch – until the smell hits ya.

I'm talking about the unlucky few who experience a violent death – a death so quick and unexpected; the eyes have no opportunity to close. Stare into the colorless eyes of one of these folks and you get the sense that they're reading your mind; sending your deepest and darkest secrets to the afterlife to be filed away and used against you when you finally make your arrival. Whenever I find myself in this situation (and that's been more than I care to admit) I have a tendency to control what I'm thinking. No need to give the afterlife a head start. It would be like walking into a job interview after they already ran a background check. They have the upper hand before you even get started.

I flip open my cell to get the time. One o'clock sharp. Just a little over three hours of daylight left. I'm not taking part in this year's hunting festivities. I stopped hunting a while back. I just lost interest.

Today I'm on duty. I just got the call from dispatch of a man lying dead at the base of a tree on this side of the mountain. The caller told our dispatcher that we could find the dead man just off of Johnson Trail about one hundred yards west of the first bend.

I won't be requiring any additional directions to locate this alleged sighting. I can't tell you how many hundreds of times I've been down this trail. I know exactly where this guy is; if he's even there at all.

Within minutes, I arrive at the bend in the trail and park my state-owned Jeep in between two towering oak trees. I make a quick exit and use the large side-view mirror to make sure my uniform is up to speed. I'll be the first officer on this one. If there's truly a dead man lying to my left, I'm sure everyone and their brother will eventually make their way down to take a peek. I will need to look my best.

Just as I finish adjusting a crooked nametag, my department radio activates and a familiar voice transmits over the airways.

"367, are you on scene yet?"

I pick up the mic.

"10-4 just pulled up. I'll let you know what we have here in a few minutes."

"10-4"

The concerned voice on the other end is that of my boss. We don't get many dead body complaints up in these parts, so all ears are tuned to my channel this afternoon.

I start into the woods and weave my way through the huge oaks and mountain laurel that cover the floor of this forest. There are trails going every which way, put down by hundreds of deer who call this home. About a hundred and fifty yards into the familiar terrain, I stop to survey the area. This is where my father used to hunt. Like me, he has retired from the game as well. No longer do we possess the desire to partake in the annual pilgrimage. Not quite sure what happened to the desire. After awhile, it just became more of a job than a passion.

As for myself, I never really got into the whole after-the-hunt thing. The part where you have to gut the deer and then drag the damn thing miles back to the truck. If you're lucky enough to survive that without heart failure, then you had the forty-mile ride back to the house to look forward to. Once at the house, you had the task of hanging the brut up while the wife is yelling "you are not cutting that thing up in my garage." It's funny how that works. They never set foot in the garage but can produce a signed, notarized deed of ownership at the drop of a hat upon the arrival of a dead animal.

After some serious negotiations, usually involving future back rubs or flowers, you finally get started on the butchering process only to find the skin is frozen to the meat. Two hours later you finally get the skin off and the meat cut up. This doesn't include packaging and labeling the meat, along with hauling it down stairs to a waiting freezer. It's no wonder why I don't hunt anymore. I think about this every time I go to my local butcher in town and order some steaks. I select what I want and they hand it to me. Sign me up!

I continue my stalk into the woods until I reach the far edge of the ravine. Deer seldom walk down the center of any depression in the land. They like to concentrate on the edges where they have a good vantage point from up high so a quick exit can be made from any impending danger.

Keeping that in mind, I start to look around for my reported dead hunter. I know I'm close. There are no clues to tell me I'm close – just intuition I guess. A few seconds go by and I see a large oak tree to my left. Just above the mountain laurel is what appears to be a backpack hanging from a tree limb a few feet off the ground. I immediately start toward the foreign object. In the back of my mind, I'm hoping the evidence I just found is that of the deceased. If it's not, I'll have some apologies to dish out to a hunter for disturbing his spot. Less than a minute later, I get my wish.

"367 to base. I'm gonna need Hanson down here."

"367, this is Hanson. What do we have?"

"What we didn't want to find."

CHAPTER 3

"Hey Mark, did you see the size of the holes in this guy's chest?"

"Marvin, how many times do I have to tell you not to call me by my first name while we're on duty? I don't want the other officers to think I play favorites."

"But you don't, so I don't know why you worry so much about it."

"Because I do and I'm your boss. So if you want to continue your employment here..."

"Okay – Okay, I got it, Sergeant Hanson. It just sounds so, formal."

"Humor me Riggs – Please?"

"Okay, but did you hear me? Look at these holes in this guy."

The man lying before me is dead: dead as they come. It's one of those deaths where you don't even check for a pulse. Just the sight of him is all the confirmation you need. The pool of blood he is sitting in is another big giveaway, along with the fact that blood and drool are hanging from his mouth.

The guy appears to have been an average 'Joe' in his mid 30s but I can't be too sure with all that face paint he's wearing. I'm confident about one thing though: This guy was serious about his hunting. I can tell from the top quality overalls he's wearing, which he has nicely accessorized with a pair of waterproof "Red Wing" hunting boots. Nothing but the best for this dead guy.

I step forward with a purpose and begin a closer examination of the scene. The corpse is sitting upright with his back against a leaning oak tree. His head is slumped forward with his chin buried into his chest. Three holes from a large caliber rifle are present on his left ribcage. Blood from his wounds have long spewed from his body. A dried trail of the red liquid is observed starting from the chest cavity and has traveled all the way to the soft, leafy ground he is sitting on. The amount of blood loss is tremendous. There has to be at least two maybe three pints lying underneath him. The dead man's compound bow is lying to his right: another item that indicates a serious hunter. A "Martin" compound with all the necessary toys attached. A weapon like this can easily go for five-hundred bucks or more at any local hunting shop.

As I continue to make notes for my report, Hanson is standing behind me watching my every move. I gaze at the scene, becoming almost hypnotized by clues that don't make sense. It catches Hanson's attention.

"What are you staring at Marvin?"

"There are some things here not adding up – not making sense."

"Like what?"

"Well for one, look at these entry wounds. Check out the diameter of these holes. They're huge.

Hanson walks around me and bends down to get a closer look at the guy's ribcage.

"You're right Marvin; they're bigger than your normal 130-gran bullet from any .270 or .306 rifle I've ever seen.

"I know. And wouldn't you think that anyone shot with a gun that can fire a round of this size would have a total of six holes in them.

"Why six?" Hanson asks.

"Well, three going in and three coming out. There are no exit wounds anywhere on this guy. Three shots from this gun should have blown his entire left side wide open.

"True" Hanson nods in agreement.

"And another thing, check out his bow. What do you see?"

"It's a nice one, that's for sure" Hanson says.

"Yeah, I see that but what's missing?"

Hanson looks over the bow lying just to the victim's right. He fails to come up with an answer to my question and his eyes suggest he's somewhat irritated with me. He has every reason to be. I'm the one in training and here I am quizzing the teacher. I guess that would irritate me as well. But I'm not your normal student. I've done this work before and Hanson knows that.

"Okay Marvin, I give."

"There's no arrow notched on the bowstring. I used to bow hunt a lot and I never went into the woods without an arrow notched and ready."

"Good observation Marvin."

"And one more things Mark: This guy doesn't have a hunting license pinned to his back. Where did that go?

"Now I did notice that. Just make sure you put all that in your report. I'm sure the detective will appreciate it."

"I doubt it. I'm sure he'll find something wrong with it?"

"I know you don't get along with him Marvin but he is a good detective and he means well."

"Means well? Are you kidding? He's an asshole. Everyone knows it. And for some unknown reason, he's got a huge hard-on for me."

Just as I finish bashing the only homicide detective we have in these parts, I hear a man shouting from the top of the ridge.

"Hey; I know you guys aren't contaminating my scene."

I look in the direction of the obnoxious sound and see Mr. 'Means Well' walking toward us. Detective Leroy Gates. A man who's tenure with the Pennsylvania Game Commission spans more than thirty years. I've heard he started off as a patrolman like myself and worked his way through the ranks, which confirms the old adage: "Screw up and move up."

Gates is somewhere in his mid 50s and as crabby as any man I've ever met. From what information I've been able to gather through the rumor mill, he lives by himself in a mobile home on the other side of the mountain. He's kind of a survivalist so-to-speak. The type of guy who raises his own cattle for meat, his own chickens for eggs, and he even has a windmill on his property to generate some of his own electricity. The report is that he was married a long time ago but no one seems to know much about her. You gotta wonder who in their right mind would hook up with this jewel.

Now I don't claim to work for the circus but if I had to guess, I would say Mr. Gates weighs in the area of three hundred and fifty pounds. I'd be in a bad mood too, if I had to carry that much weight around day after day.

I remember growing up in a family that had its share of overweight folks. I recall an aunt whose name escapes me right now. The only time I ever saw her was during holiday dinners at my grandmother's house. Each year I would watch her attempt to enter grandma's house and I swear she had to negotiate the doorway. She was as wide as she was tall. My dad would always elbow me in the ribs when she arrived. He told me on a number of occasions that if you don't take care of yourself, you could end up like that. That visual has stuck with me like glue. There isn't a week goes by that I don't conduct a feet check. That's where you standing up against a wall and without moving your head, look down. If you can't see your feet, then it's time to cut back on the Twinkies.

Gates reaches the scene quickly due to the fact that he was walking down hill. He stops to my left and stares me down as if I did something wrong.

"Mr. Riggs, what are you doing to my crime scene?'

I return the stare just to let him know I am not intimidated by his presence here. Besides, I was here first. It's my scene for now.

"I'm taking notes for my report Gates and have not contaminated your scene. And just for your information, I've done your job before so I know a little of what you do."

"Yeah, I know all about you City Boy. I guess you came up here to the mountains so you can show us country folks how to do things. Is that right?"

"You know Gates; I don't take what you say personally. You treat everybody like shit. I can't believe they keep you around. I can tell you this much, if you were working in Milwaukee, I don't care how good you are, you'd be nothing but a memory. Now let's get down to business here. We have a dead man whose family is going to want an explanation of why their husband or son went out for a day of hunting and ended up dead."

"I agree Marvin." Hanson interjects. "Do you have everything for your initial report?"

"Yeah, I got it."

"Okay. Gates, the scene is yours. Marvin, take off."

"Yes Sergeant Hanson. And Gates, before I forget, I got your 'Boy' right here."

Not waiting for a response from anyone, I walk around the recently deceased and make my way up the ridge where my patrol vehicle is parked. I can't help but wonder why Gates has such a problem with me. He picks on everyone, but especially me. My mere presence seems to set him into bitch mode. I can only assume he's jealous because I only have one ass.

CHAPTER 4

I'm now sitting in the west parking lot, ten minutes removed from my Gates encounter. In order to keep vehicle traffic off this mountain, the state erected a huge steel gate. I would guess the structure to be over thirty-years old, with a minimum of twenty coats of paint covering it. This heavy gauge barrier and I have become close friends over the past several weeks. It represents where we are as a country and the lengths we'll take to preserve and protect the innocence of nature. I have often believed that gates and locks are only a mirage. They're not a fool-proof means of keeping destructive forces at bay. If evil wants to get in, it'll find a way. The only thing locks and gates can really do is keep honest people honest. We really can't ask anything more from them.

I am one of only three people in this world who have a key to this particular gate. I say who has access and who doesn't. This mirage represents the boundary between civilization and the great outdoors. A world filed with trees, brush, and wildlife - everything that is pure and natural. It's my job to make sure it stays that way; and I take that responsibility very seriously.

It's three o'clock in the afternoon, according to my new Sanyo phone. I look around and observe more than twenty vehicles parked here today. The first day of bow season usually draws a pretty good crowd. Every one of these folks walked back here; except for me. My vehicle is the only one allowed to penetrate this sacred land. Game Wardens have that privilege.

It was just last year that I was back at my old house in Wisconsin. My youngest daughter had just left the house to take on this nasty world and carve a life out for herself. The last couple of years have not been easy for either of my kids. They've had a ton of questions about what happened. A lot of them I can't answer. For those of you who've been without cable or in a coma, let me get you up to speed on what took place here.

It started back in 06' when my father, brother, and I were on our annual hunting trip right here at Martin's Hill. That year Dad shot a nice buck, and there was talk later that the rack might just score out to be a world's record. But when we went to retrieve the huge brut, someone else beat us to it. A female hunter had already staked claim to the buck and went so far as to take a shot at us when we attempted to take it back. Needless to say, we got out of there and in a hurry.

To make a long story short, the woman was later found dead at the exact spot where Dad and I had confronted her. The buck was returned to my father and we all went about our business with a great story to tell.

Five weeks later, I got the call while at work. Dad was shot and killed in his work shop. His head had been blown off, shot at point blank range. I immediately flew up and started learning things about my father that would endanger my life and everyone around me.

It seems Dad secretly took on a part-time job hauling whitetail deer from the east coast to a ranch here in Bedford. He'd been doing this for cash for several years until one day; he found he was not only hauling deer, but diamonds. Diamonds from South Africa were being smuggled into the country. The smugglers were concealing the jewels inside the deer's antlers. Dad found this out and immediately discontinued this employment with the company without giving a two weeks notice. Guess that wasn't good enough.

I eventually got possession of the huge buck. It wasn't long after and all these strange people started paying me way-too-much attention. I thought they were after the huge buck because it was potentially a world record, which would mean hundreds of thousands of dollars for its owner. I didn't learn about the diamonds until I was forced off the road in a suburb near here and shot when I attempted to flee. But I survived, thanks to my father.

That's right. My father blew his brains out before he could do the same to me. My father, who I thought was buried in a grave back in Pennsylvania, was alive and well. The guy killed back in Dad's shop was one of his students from the college where he taught woodworking. He was the same age, same height, and same weight as my father. The police just assumed it was him.

Dad kept his survival a secret and shadowed me, until my pursuer made his move. He knew they'd come after me. Since then, Dad has kept his dead secret, out of fear of what the authorities would do with him if he came forward. Only three people in the world know he's alive, and we aim to keep in that way.

So with no wife to nag me to death and no kids emptying my wallet, I suddenly found myself alone with not much purpose in life. One can only go on so many bike rides. It's funny how that works. You bitch and complain while they're here and suddenly they're gone and you miss them. A friend once told me, we always think the grass is greener somewhere else but in reality; it's just a different shade.

A few weeks into my exile, I began pondering my options for the future. I was lucky in the fact that I could go anywhere I wanted. Thoughts of going out west to Arizona were quickly dismissed. I couldn't imagine staring at dirt and sand all day. Then there was Wyoming and the endless miles of mountain ranges along with the lack of human habitation. But the fear of grizzly bears ended that fantasy. It was Pennsylvania that kept me smiling. I couldn't think of a finer place to live out my years. Martin's Hill would be heaven on earth for me.

But then reality hit. I'm approaching fifty and still need to work. My investments in pet rocks and hand-held adding machines haven't quite panned out. And then one day I got an idea. I could be a game warden. I have a law enforcement background and my love for the outdoors would just be the icing on the cake. What department wouldn't hire me with my qualifications?

So one day I picked up the phone and called that Hanson fellow: The game warden that crossed my path a few years ago when my dad and I were shot at. He was the officer who handled our case and as luck would have it, I still had his business card in my wallet.

A few weeks later, I took some time off work from the bank and flew out to meet him. He was now a Sergeant and we hit it off right from the start. After a few phone calls, an application, and a two-weeks notice to the bank, I was attending the game warden academy. Two months later, I graduated and got assigned to patrol the Martin's Hill area. The same area I grew up in. The job I had always dreamed of. I think Hanson had something to do with that but he refuses to admit it. I owe him a great deal.

I sold just about everything I owned and moved to Bedford. Since then, Hanson and I have become good friends and great partners out in the field. But he's all business when it comes to this line of work and never misses an opportunity to remind me who's in charge. I normally don't take that too well but again, I owe him a great deal so I entertain it – to a point.

He even took the time to help me move into my apartment and also introduced me to my current girlfriend. Hanson and I share everything, except the fact that my father is still alive. Dad lives only a few miles away in a very secluded location, which was his plan all along. I stop by about every other week to check on him. I have to be careful though. I shudder to think what would happen if Hanson ever found out the old man is still among the living.

After locking the gate back up, I enter my Jeep Liberty and crank up the engine. I pause for a moment and wonder what our deceased friend drove here. One of these twenty vehicles belongs to him. I'm sure Gates will find the man's wallet soon and run a check through DMV, which will instantly tell us what make and model to look for; that is if they find a wallet.

"367 to Hanson" I holler out over the airways.

"367 go ahead."

"I'm down here in the parking lot. Do we know what vehicle we need to secure yet?"

"No we don't Riggs. There is no wallet or ID on our subject. Can you hang out there until the parking lot empties? We'll have to play last-man-standing to ID this guy."

"What about his hunting license? We can run the number through the computer."

"Marvin, he doesn't have one on him - remember?"

"That's right, I forgot."

"Can you hang over this evening?" Hanson asks.

"10-4. I'll let you know as soon as the lot empties."

CHAPTER 5

The digital clock on my dashboard reads five-twenty. The sun has already made its final appearance for the day and has quietly retired for the evening. I've been sitting here across the street since three o'clock, watching the parking lot empty out one vehicle at a time; with most of the hunters going home empty-handed. No shame in that. Hunting is about spending a quality day in the woods. Just because you didn't bag the big buck, doesn't make you less of a man – or woman. It does make for less work when you get home.

Hanson and Gates are still on top of the mountain. It takes time to process a crime scene, even though we're not quite sure a crime has even been committed. But in this business you assume the worst, just in case the worst did occur.

I recall one day when I was working patrol back in the early 90's in Florida. I had only been with the department for a few months when I was dispatched to an apartment where a landlord had just found one of his tenants lying dead inside. The medical people got there first and confirmed the lack of a heart beat and brain activity. Lacking brain activity myself, I arrived on scene a few minutes later and found an elderly man lying face-up on a bed in a corner bedroom. He was wearing dress pants, dress shoes, and a neatly-pressed dress shirt. Since it was a Monday, I made the assumption that he was getting ready for church yesterday morning and had a heart attack or stroke.

Without searching the room for any evidence to the contrary, I called the station and reported the death as natural and summoned for the funeral home to respond to pick up the body. The hearse arrived within a few minutes and I escorted them to the room. I walked outside to get some fresh air. The death smell was taking over the room and I could feel my stomach churning from the odor. A few minutes later, one of the funeral personnel exited and got my attention.

"Officer, you need to take a look at what we found."

I followed the young man back inside who led me to a small table in the corner of the living room. On the table were three hand-written letters, which were each addressed to his three daughters. I also observed a prepaid funeral card and an empty bottle of prescription medication sitting next to the letters. After perusing one of the letters, it was crystal clear that the old guy had committed suicide. If I would have taken a few minutes to look around, I would have not suffered the embarrassment of having to send the funeral home back and call for the coroner, along with my supervisor. The incident taught me a valuable lesson: Believe nothing you hear and only half of what you see.

That philosophy has served me well over the years. The words were ringing loud and clear in my head while looking at the body earlier today. I had to keep reminding myself that it may look like someone shot this guy – but did they? I'm still not sure what I saw up there. A hunter with no license, no arrow notched in his bow and three holes in the guy's chest with no exit wounds. Just doesn't add up.

———————

It's now five forty-five and dark outside. I'm staring at two vehicles still sitting in the parking lot. One is a newer model Dodge Durango and the other a Chevy Silverado. I key-up the two-way radio:

"367"

"367 go ahead."

"Need you to run two Pennsylvania plates through DMV."

"10-4 go ahead."

"First one is LPN-199 and the second is RBG-332."

"10-4 stand-by.

While I wait for a reply, Hanson calls me.

"367"

"367 go head."

Gates and I are finished up here. We're going to exit from the other side of the mountain. Not as steep on that side. Don't want to get the hearse stuck up here. Do you have a vehicle left in the parking lot?"

"I've got two – a Durango and a Silverado. Dispatch is running the plates for me now."

"It's a little late to be hunting," says Hanson.

"I agree. Maybe one of these guys stuck one late and running behind with getting down off the mountain."

"367" says dispatch.

"367 go ahead."

"Your Silverado comes back registered to a Brian Morgan out of Ridgeway and the Durango to a Claudio Santiago out of Huntington."

We now know who our victim is. The face on the man in the woods had no Hispanic characteristics whatsoever. He was a white guy through and through.

"367 to Sergeant Hanson – did you catch that?"

"10-4. I'm sending the crime scene tech your way for processing. As soon as she gets there, you go home."

"10-4 thanks."

The crime scene tech should be here in a few minutes. Good time to step out and have a cigarette. The state won't let you smoke inside their vehicles anymore. There's nothing more relaxing than cruising down the highway with the driver's side window cracked, and the smoke from a quality menthol cigarette evaporating into oblivion. It wasn't that long ago a person could smoke anywhere they wanted. I can remember back in the early 90s helping out in our dispatch center at the police department. I would sit at a desk and smoke a pack without thinking about the harm I was doing to myself and the people around me. If you were a non-smoker, you just had to put up with it.

Even though I smoke, I am glad there are rules to keep us smokers in check. It wasn't fair to those who make a conscious effort to avoid this nasty habit. I often wonder how many non-smokers have died over the years from our lack of concern. The rules do help keep my consumption under control, along with the five-dollar a pack price tag that now goes along with them. I shudder to think how much money I've spent over the years on these things.

I'm halfway finished with my cigarette when I catch sight of a pair of headlights heading down the mountain. It must be the crime scene tech. Her arrival signals the end of a long day for me. I know it's a "her" because she is the only tech we have that works this area. It's just one of the many advantages of living here. When you're the only tech assigned to the entire county, you can be assured there's not much crime to deal with. What a difference coming from where I used to live in Florida. If my memory serves me correctly, I think they had a team of thirty techs working my county.

Her name is April and she stops at the yellow gate. Being the gentleman that I am, I walk over and open the gate for her. She drives through and I direct her to the Silverdo. April promptly parks and exits her vehicle.

"Hello Marvin?"

"Hi April"

"Thanks for getting the gate for me."

"No problem."

"Which vehicle am I processing?"

"The Silverado."

"What's up with the Durango?"

"I'm not sure. Just a late hunter I guess. Do you have any keys for this thing?"

"They found a set of keys in the victim's front pocket. I guess we'll find out soon enough if the Silverado is our vehicle."

April secures a set of keys from her pocket and inserts them into the driver's side door keyhole. With a quick jolt to the left, the door unlocks and entry is gained without having to break a thing.

"That's my cue. Catch ya later, April."

"Take care Riggs. Tell Mandi I said Hi."

"I'll do that."

I make my left out of the lot and head down the mountain toward home. It'll feel good to kick my feet up and pass-out on the couch. A power nap is just what the doctor ordered. Hopefully Mandi won't mind if I spend an evening to myself. That's the advantage of having a girlfriend in lieu of a spouse. You have the option to make such a decision.

CHAPTER 6

"367!"

My department walkie-talkie is up so loud that the sound of my own call number startles me. So much so that it causes me to spill my hot cup of coffee all over my nicely pressed white shirt. I'll be spending the rest of the day hearing "You spilled coffee on your shirt." And I'll probably smirk and reply with, "I'll make a note."

"367 go ahead" I blurt with a disgusted tone.

"We've received a complaint of a large crowd gathering in the west lot of Martin's Hill."

"10-4, and the problem?"

"Not sure. I suspect its PETA again."

"10-4. I'll be in route."

It's the day after the body was found. My power nap turned into an all-nighter. After picking up a sub at my local deli, along with a pint of cold slaw and chips, I went straight home and consumed these vital nutrients in record time. I managed to get halfway through an episode of "COPS" before passing out on the couch. I never regained consciousness until five this morning. I'm surprised that Mandi didn't call or come over. Some girlfriend I have.

I'm also surprised that I slept so well after spending a good half hour hovering over that body yesterday. I've hovered over many a deceased in my police days, and the image of each one is permanently engraved into my skull. I can remember every detail from what they were wearing to their cause of death. It stays with you. You can't get rid of it. All you can do is rationalize that this is part of the circle of life and move on. I guess for me it's so automatic that I don't even have to remind myself anymore.

I proceed down Richmond Road while obeying the posted speed limit. I don't have to but I'm in no hurry to get to this call. There's no one dying that I know of and no need to put other lives in danger for some PETA demonstration. Besides, I need a few minutes to plan a strategy.

Being the new guy in the game warden business, everything I do is being scrutinized. From how I complete my daily activity reports to handling disturbance calls like this one; everything is documented in triplicate. I haven't heard any complaints lately and they have been letting up on me a little for the past two weeks. The only one complaining is Gates. Not sure what I'm going to do about that – probably nothing.

If my Jeep was equipped with a boring machine, the west parking lot would only be a mile away. But they don't call it a mountain because it's flat. And since all the helicopters were checked out this morning, I'm content to take the ten mile journey around to get there. They pay me by the hour so we're good.

Television is the only information I have to draw from regarding PETA. The media always shows these radical individuals who will stop at nothing to protect the lives of every living thing that occupies this earth. In a way I kind of admire that. They're not hurting anyone. No one ever dies as a result of their protests. I can only imagine what they might be doing in the west lot. Maybe a hunter has dragged a deer down to his vehicle and they won't let him load it up on the bed of his truck or something like that. I'll need to be cordial and diplomatic when I get there. Wouldn't you know it; the two characteristics I do not possess.

I round the bend at Gap Road and see a gathering of people in the lot directly ahead of me. I ease into the gravel parking area so not to alarm anyone. A fast and abrupt entry would put folks on the defensive. I don't have enough energy or handcuffs to arrest all of them at one time.

"367"

"367" the dispatcher acknowledges.

"I'm on location."

"Are you going to need a backup unit? If so I have 210 available."

"Not at this time. I'll advise."

"210" is Hanson. I only have to address him as such on the radio. We're such a small department that I'm not quite sure of the reasoning behind assigning each one of us a number. I believe it's a combination of things. It's probably easier for the dispatchers to keep track of our activities by jotting down a number in lieu of a name. Another reason might be that everyone and their brother has a scanner these days. When you take away people's freedoms for a living, you have a tendency to piss them off. No need giving out your name over the airways, letting everyone know where you're at.

I exit my Jeep and stop for a moment to assess the activities of strangers before me. A group of about fifteen folks are gathered around an old Ford LTD station wagon, carrying signs and banners declaring the killing of anything as an abomination. Inside the circle of doom is an elderly man sitting on his tailgate, yelling something at the demonstrators. The man is in full camouflage but has no bow in hand. He is visibly upset and when he finally makes eye contact with my uniform, he immediately cuts through the crowd and straight for my location.

"Officer, my name is Elmer P Goodman and these folks won't let me hunt" he yells as he gasps for air.

Not sure why he feels the importance to tell me his middle initial but so be it.

"What do you mean they won't let you hunt?"

"I mean what I just said. Every damn time I start up the mountain, these yahoos follow me. I don't mind the company – don't get me wrong. But they won't quit yelling and screaming. They're scaring all the deer. I know who they are. They're that PETO group that's been coming around here for the past couple of years. I guess it's my turn to get harassed. I'm a tax payer officer and a good American. I should be able to go hunting in peace. I've paid my dues."

I listen as the elderly man continues on this rant about his service to our country and what rights he should have. I'm guessing this guy is somewhere in his mid to late 70s and I'm hoping he doesn't vapor lock on me before he finishes. I want him to get the frustration out of his system, and venting is the best way to do it. But this guy has a lot to say. I finally cut him off at the part where he jumped off the boat and onto the shores of Normandy.

"Okay, Mr. Goodman, I understand your complaint and you have every right to hunt in peace. Just give me a few minutes and I'll get you started up the mountain – alone. And by the way, it's PETA, not PETO."

The old man says nothing. He steps aside as I make my way toward the group of individuals who I'm blaming for spilling my coffee and causing me a premature trip to the drycleaners. As I eye the crowd, I'm looking for someone in charge; someone who will step forward and take some responsibility. I don't see anyone taking a lead role here. No suits or ties or briefcases to indicate who is running this show. Everyone is wearing jeans and jackets. I guess I'll have to ask. Surely someone here wants to come forward and claim to be the chosen one.

"Who's in charge here?" I ask the thirty eyes who are staring at the badge pinned on my jacket.

There is a second of uncomfortable silence as all eyes hone in on an individual standing in the back. I adjust my head to the left and watch as a woman dressed like a dude emerges.

"I'm in charge officer. What seems to be the problem?"

"Well I have a complaint that you're harassing this gentleman."

"You mean that old guy over there who wants to kill innocent creatures? I don't see a problem here at all – Riggs."

"Don't play with me ma'am. You know what the problem is here. And you will address me as Officer Riggs."

"Yeah whatever" she mutters with an irritated tone.

To say her attitude is beginning to annoy me would be an understatement. I feel as if someone just struck one of my kids. But I'm not in a position where I can lash out at those who disrespect me or my authority. My ego is larger than most, but my responsibility for this uniform and the State of Pennsylvania is even larger. I will need to maintain my composure.

"Ma'am, what is your name?"

"That's none of your damn business officer."

Okay – enough of the maintaining my composure thing.

Sensing a potential problem, I reach for my radio mic.

"367"

"367 go ahead."

"Please have 210 respond to this location."

"10-4"

My ego maybe large, but common sense reigns supreme in my world. I have a group of fifteen folks (both men and women) in front of me with a leader who thinks the law is on her side. If I have to arrest this woman, I could have a problem with the other fourteen who believe they have an obligation to come to her rescue. I'm good at what I do, but I can't take fourteen at once. That would be as dumb as bringing a knife to a gun fight.

With my index finger pointed directly at the woman's eyes, I initiate the demand phase of our meeting.

"Ma'am, please step over here so you and I can talk in private."

The woman stands motionless for a few seconds. She crosses her arms and looks behind her to make sure her followers haven't left her high and dry. They are all standing firm.

"Ma'am, I'm only going to say this one more time. You step over here so we can talk about what is taking place here or you will be arrested, along with anyone else who would like to try me."

"Is that so?" she says.

"You can count on it ma'am."

"Who is 210?"

"210 is our swat team."

The woman slowly and reluctantly uncrosses her arms and walks over. She is not a mountain girl or anything of the sort. She is an attractive woman in her mid 30s with blonde hair, blue eyes, and a bad attitude toward law enforcement. She smells good though.

We are now inches apart as I lean into her face.

"Now what is your name?"

"Candace."

"Okay Candace, here's the deal. The old guy paid $17.95 for a hunting license this year. He has the right and the backing of this state to go hunting and be left alone. I understand what you're trying to accomplish and this practice is only going to end with someone getting hurt."

"Yeah, the deer." She says.

"No, not the deer. You!"

"Candace. I do not have the time or the patience to baby-sit this the entire day, and I'm not going to. If you want to demonstrate your displeasure with the harvesting of these animals, please do so. You can stay right here in the parking lot if you wish, but you will not follow any hunters into the woods. Are we clear?"

"You can't enforce that once you leave."

"No Candace you're right – but he can."

I look over at Elmer who is leaning on my Jeep working on a Marlboro.

"Hey Elmer!"

"Yes sir."

"Do me a favor, will ya."

"What's that?"

"Grab your bow and start up the trail to your hunting spot. And if any of these folks decide to tag along, you have my authority to turn around, notch an arrow, and stick one right in their chest. Got it?"

"You got it boss."

Elmer rushes over to his station wagon as quickly as a seventy year old man can. He grabs his gear and heads up the trail with me and Candace watching, and the rest of her entourage watching her. I turn and walk back to my Jeep, deliberately ignoring Candace all together and hoping to God almighty that my false intimidation works.

As I reach my door, I see Hanson rounding the bend and speed into the lot. He slams on the breaks and comes to a sliding stop directly beside me.

"What's up Marvin?"

"I believe it's handled now."

I then hear Candice's voice behind me.

"Is that your swat team?"

"Swat team? Marvin what's she talking about?"

CHAPTER 7

I pull into the Spring Haven Apartments after a long day of work. This complex is the place I now call home: One-bedroom efficiency with plenty of room for me and my stuff. It's all I'll ever need as long as I stay single. Even though I live here by myself, the complex gives me two parking spaces. When I pulled in this evening, I find another car sitting in my extra space, much to my delight.

The gray Ford Focus belongs to my girlfriend, Mandi. She's a dispatcher I met two weeks after starting with the game commission. I remember the day we met back in the briefing room. She was just hired and the supervisor in charge of the communications area was walking her around making the required introductions. There was something about the way she said hello to me that got my attention. Her handshake was as soft and gentle as any greeting that I'd ever received. She was instantly interested in me, which doesn't happen very often in my world.

After asking around and finding out she was a single lady in her mid 30s, it didn't take me long to ask her out after work for a cup of coffee. We immediately hit it off and haven't stopped seeing each other since.

Mandi is about my height with shoulder length brunette hair and a little on the chunky side, but not fat. She has a beautiful complexion and a smile that can make a blind man weak at the knees. She has a place on the other side of town - an apartment much like mine. We get together a few nights a week for cooking, communication, and curling up on the couch with a good DVD in the player. We have talked about moving in together and save us both some money. But we've come to the conclusion that everything is working so well right now, so why screw it up.

Mandi and I haven't slept together yet either. We really haven't discussed the possibility and I don't want to be the one to bring it up. I've always been under the impression that sex is a decision left to the woman. They are the ones who have to submit to us men and usually do things to make us happy even though they are really not comfortable about it. I respect that.

I exit my Jeep and hit the lock button on my key chain. The double beep echoes through the parking lot telling the whole City of Bedford that I'm home. I walk to my front door, which just happens to be my only door, and through the kitchen window I see Mandi standing behind the counter working on something. We may not live together but we did exchange keys several weeks ago. I guess the relationship is progressing as well as can be expected.

As I open the door, she looks over and gives me a stare like I was just found on a deserted island after being missing for a year or so.

"Hey good-look'n."

"Hi Marvin. I heard about the dead guy up in the mountain. Did you see him?"

Mandi shuffles over and puts her arms around my neck. With the precision of a married woman, she gives a quick kiss. Most of the time her kisses are kind of long, but today she must want to talk.

"Yeah I saw him. I actually spent quite a bit of time with him as a matter of fact."

"How did he look? Was he all creepy and gooey like?

I release my grip and step back.

"Have you ever seen a dead person?"

"Not in real life – just on television."

"So you've never really seen a real dead person then."

"I guess not. Marvin, you have to tell me. What do they look like?"

"It all depends on how they die. I take it you were off today. I didn't hear your voice over the airwaves."

"Marvin dammit, answer my question."

"Okay. The guy was shot three times in the side and there was a lot of blood."

"Three holes huh? Were they like bullet size holes or real small ones?"

"Actually Mandi, they were the largest bullet holes I've ever seen on a body."

"So how do you know he was shot?"

"I guess he was. What else would have caused such damage? I'm no expert but I'd put money down on it. Why are you so intrigued about this?"

"I have always wanted to be an investigator and go on the hunt for a murderer or serial killer."

"Whoa, slow down Mandi. We don't even know if the guy was murdered. It could be just a hunting accident. That's the most important thing you have to keep in mind when investigating a death. You can't assume what you see is true. I had a detective tell me one day: Believe only half of what you see and nothing you hear."

"I guess you're right. Are you hungry?"

"I sure am."

"Good. I made a cheese and broccoli casserole."

"Cool. Are you going to be coming over unannounced more often."

"Maybe."

"Very cool."

Mandi and I sit down at the small kitchen table I got at the local Goodwill store, and dive into the casserole. It is delicious, and I even have some left over for lunch tomorrow.

After eating and some clean-up, we retire to the couch for some much needed snuggling time. I find it funny that when I was married twenty years ago, this was something I considered boring. Why would anyone just want to lie around on the couch for hours without the promise of wild kinky sex? Now it's my favorite thing to do. No heavy breathing, no exchange of bodily fluids, no warm wash cloth on standby. Just soft intimate closeness with a special someone. But if she wants to have sex, I sure as hell ain't going to turn her down. I may be in my late forties, but I'm not dead – yet.

The movie tonight is one that I've seen a few times, *Pirates of the Caribbean*. I do love that Jack Sparrow character. If I were a pirate, I would be exactly like him. I would live to roam the continents without a care in the world but always have a scheme up my sleeve.

After two hours of swash-buckling excitement, I stand to see Mandi out the door. It's eleven o'clock and our normal ritual on date night. But for some reason, she's is not heading for the front door. I watch as she makes her way to my bedroom.

"Where are you going?"

"I think it's time, Marvin."

"Time for what?"

"You know – time to put the seal of approval on this relationship, the notary stamp, the required postage.

"You're kidding?"

"Nope – are you interested?"

My body is ready but my mind is trying to catch up. I do want to but it's been so long. What if I suck at this? My nerves are taking over and causing me to hesitate. I can't say no. She'll be hurt if I refuse. I have to go through with this.

"Marvin, will you be coming?"

"Hopefully!"

I ease down the hallway and enter my room. Mandi is not playing around with this. She's already undressed and waiting on me, lying on my bed wearing nothing more than a smile. I stare like a teenage boy getting a glimpse at his first set of tits from the cover of darkness. I always thought of Mandi as kind of chunky but her body is well proportioned. I now have confirmation of that and strip as well in record time. With a total disregard for any dignity, I jump into bed and prepare for the festivities. As I lean forward to kiss this beautiful woman, the phone rings.

"Who the hell could that be?" I say out loud.

I lean over Mandi and look at the caller ID screen. I recognize the number as being that of the office. I have to answer it. If I don't, they'll come to the house to get me and then I'll have to explain why I did not answer the phone. If that doesn't work, they'll page me until my battery dies. No getting around it.

I look at Mandi who knows I must.

"Hello!"

"Marvin. It's Hanson. Are you busy?"

"I was gett'n there. Why?"

"I hear someone else with you Marvin. Who is it?"

"Well seeing that it's really none of your business, I just happen to have Mandi over this evening. Is that okay with you?"

"What do I care? You need to get dressed, Marvin?"

"Why?"

"We just found another dead hunter."

CHAPTER 8

Walking down Johnson Trail at ten o'clock in the evening is no small task. The night air is moist making the rocks on this trail quite treacherous. I've almost busted my ass several times making my way down this mountain. Without a flashlight, I'd probably be no better off than our new dead friend.

I make it down to the base of the hill and the forest has turned into a parking lot. Unlike the first body we found, I have plenty of company on this one. Hanson, Gates, and just about every senior ranking officer is here on this one. With a second body found, the media is about to have a story and the public is going to be demanding an explanation.

I arrive at the edge of the yellow crime scene tape that is flapping in the night breeze. Huge floodlights illuminate the scene, making the dead man even more gruesome than he already is. I stand about twenty feet away from the body and can smell the odor of decay already. The man is Hispanic and is sitting against a tree just like the guy we found this afternoon.

I notice Hanson working closely with April; making sure she gets all the pictures and evidence they're going to need. Hanson secures his two-way from his belt clip.

"367?"

Now I could just holler over and let him know that I'm here, but what fun would that be. I grab my two-way as well.

"367 go ahead."

"Marvin – where are you at?"

"I'm standing right behind you."

Hanson turns around and is not laughing. I'm met with look of disgust as he returns his radio to its proper resting place. Hanson quickly walks over.

"Marvin, why did you do that?"

"Do What?"

"You could have just called out to me."

"Yeah I could have. So we have another body lying up here."

"I don't get it Marvin. We have not had any hunting accidents up here in over thirty years, and now two in one day."

"I've got a good idea what the guys name is."

"Who - the dead guy?"

"Yes the dead guy, who else. Claudio Santiago."

"Now how in the hell do you know that."

"Remember those tag numbers I ran on those two vehicles this morning?"

"Yeah."

"Well the second vehicle came back to a Hispanic male and that vehicle is still sitting down in the west parking lot."

"That's right. I forgot about that. I'll have April go down and process it when she finishes here.

"So, Hanson, why am I here."

"Cause this is your area buddy. And the brass is asking questions about who is responsible for the patrol around here. Thought it best to come out and make an appearance."

"They do know that my hunters wouldn't appreciate being at full draw on a nice buck, only to be spooked by a 4x4 Jeep creeping down the ravine."

"You know how politics works."

"No Mark – I don't. I work for a living."

"Okay fine. Stick to your blue-collar ethics if you want. But do get your notebook out and start taking notes for your report."

Hanson lifts the tape up and I duck down to enter this recently proclaimed sacred ground. A few steps later, I stand before the body of another hunter. I cover my nose and mouth as I lean forward to examine the three holes in the guys left ribcage, along with the three holes on his right side on this one.

"Hanson, this guy was shot too. But the bullets appear to have passed through him."

"I know, and the holes are huge just like the first victim."

I stand up and back away from the body. I am starting to taste the smell now and I can no longer stand it. I make note of the holes and find everything else eerily similar to that of the first guy (his bow lying out to his side with no arrow notched, and the sitting position of the body). I look over at Hanson.

"What are the chances of two guys hunting on the same side of the mountain getting accidentally shot by the same gun?"

"Why do you think all the brass is here Marvin?"

"I see your point."

"Don't waste a lot of time. Just get some notes and head back to your apartment. I'll need you sharp tomorrow morning at nine."

"For what?"

"They're doing the autopsy on the first guy. I want you there."

"Why do I have to be there? Gates is handling this."

"Gates has requested you be there to assist him."

"Gates said that?"

"Yeap!"

"Did he say why?"

"Nope!"

"Wow. I guess I'll be there."

CHAPTER 9

The sign on the door reads: Dr. Joseph Winger – Coroner. Behind this door is where a silent few call their workplace. These chosen few spend their eight hours cutting into human beings trying to determine how and why they died. They are the translators for those who can no longer speak - the interpreters of the afterlife. They say that dead men tell no tales. Not true. They can speak volumes if you know the language.

I turn the knob and enter a small room that resembles a waiting area at the dentists' office. A woman behind the counter greets me with a smile as she slides the glass window to her right.

"May I help you sir?"

"Yes, Marvin Riggs here to view an autopsy."

The woman promptly secures a clipboard which I can only assume has the names of those being cut open today.

"Yes Mr. Riggs. Please enter the door to my right and go to room number three. Doctor Winger is waiting on you."

"Thank you ma'am."

The door buzzes, which is my cue to enter. I thrust open the door and make my way down a cold cement hallway. The walls are painted gray with no pictures or flowers to dress up the place. A couple of air fresheners wouldn't hurt either; I can smell the dead.

As I pass by door number one, I can hear a saw cutting into something. I know from experience what it is. It's definitely bone and probably from the ribcage. I can hear the echoing sound from the chest cavity as the blade makes its way down the sternum.

I soon arrive at door number three and knock. I'm not sure if I have to announce my presence before entering but I do anyways. It's a product of good home training. A voice from within beckons me to enter without disclosing my identity. I do as instructed.

I push open the door and the smell of cold meat slaps me in the face. I guess you get used to it after awhile. No different than someone working at a chocolate factory everyday. But I sure as hell would rather smell a Hershey's special dark than this crap.

The room is as blah as the hallway. The concrete walls are painted gray, with polished metal cabinets lining the back wall. No pictures or flowers here either. I look up and see huge fluorescent lights hanging from the gray painted ceiling. All lights are aimed at the long metal table, which accents the décor in the middle of the room with the body of our first hunting victim as the centerpiece. The good doctor and Hanson stand behind him and stare at me as I approach.

"Good Morning Marvin," Hanson says.

"Well you're half right." I answer. "Where's Gates?"

"He won't be in today – called in sick. He requested you take down the information and put a report on his desk."

"He wants me to do it?

"Yeah – can you believe it?" says Hanson. "Your charm is wearing on him."

"I doubt that."

Doctor Winger steps forward and clears his throat.

"Gentleman, let's get started here. I took the liberty of beginning the autopsy early this morning and I'm glad I did, because something weird is going on with this one."

The doctor grabs a corner of the sheet covering the dead man and flips it back. Our victim is now nude and white as a ghost. His chest has been split open and the three bullet holes on the side of his chest are circle with a black marker.

With notepad and pen in hand, I draw a rough sketch of the body; making note of where exactly the three entry wounds are located on the chest. The highest hole is between the third and fourth rib. The second one is between rib four and five. And the third one completely broke rib number six. I also note that the third hole is larger in diameter than the other two.

"I see you made note of the third puncture wound Mr. Riggs," says Winger.

"Yes I did. The hole is larger."

"And what does that tell you officer."

"It tells me that this guy was either shot with two different guns or he wasn't shot at all."

"Your later observation is correct. He wasn't shot."

"Then what killed him Doc?"

"He was impaled."

"IMPALED? With what?" ask Hanson.

The doctor pauses for a moment.

"In my professional opinion, death was caused by a set of antlers."

"Antlers!" I exclaim. "What do you mean antlers?"

"I mean a male white-tail deer stuck this man in the chest while he was hunting."

"IMPOSSIBLE!" Hanson says. "Are you sure, doc?"

"Positive. I found microscopic pieces of cartilage lining all three puncher wounds and had them analyzed this morning. Without a doubt, a whitetail deer charged this guy and killed him. That's why the top wound is larger in diameter. The third point known as the ting on a set of deer antlers is customarily the largest. In all my years of doing this, I've never seen nor heard of such a thing. Deer attacking hunters – it's just not right."

I pause and reflect back when I first saw this guy in the woods. I didn't observe any signs of a struggle. I've heard about deer getting overly aggressive with hunters after using too much deer urine. But certainly he would have tried to fight off the buck in some manner.

"Hanson. Did we recover any deer lure from this guy at the scene?"

"Nope. Why?"

"I was thinking maybe we have a really horny deer on our hands and when he got a whiff of that stuff, the deer went nuts."

"As far as I know Marvin, this guy didn't have any deer scent with him."

Other ideas are going through my head but I'm not at liberty to discuss them - not in front of the doc. I don't really know who he is or if I can trust him. These are thoughts best kept close to the vest. I'll discuss them later with Hanson. I always do better when I can brainstorm with someone I know.

"So Doc, are we done here?"

"I guess so. I'm running a few lab tests, but other than that, you guys have your cause of death. I'm going to list the cause as accidental on the death certificate for now. If you come up with anything other than that, let me know."

"Will do Doctor. Thanks for the invite."

Hanson and I leave out the same door I came in. Two more doors and we enter the parking lot.

"So Marvin, what do you want to talk about?"

"How'd you know I wanted to talk?"

"I saw the look on your face and you never just ask one question."

"Okay: Let's just say this guy was hunting and a deer charged him. Do you think we'd have found him sitting up the way we did. No way. He would have been lying on the ground. And why are there no defensive wounds? I sure as hell wouldn't let something charge at me without a fight."

"Maybe he was sleeping." Hanson says.

"No way – It's the first day of hunting season. No one falls asleep on the first day. Hunters have been anticipating opening day for the past year. I remember when I went hunting on a regular basis. I was wound so tight on opening day, you'd a thought I was on crack."

"You do have a point there, Marvin."

"And another thing, why was there no arrow notched in that bow? From all accounts, this guy was experienced at this. And where's the buck lure? No one goes hunting without at least some type of cover scent. Hanson, this whole thing is just weird."

"I agree Marvin, but it's not your problem."

"But it happened on my side of the mountain."

"Do your report and hit the road. If I need another investigator, I'll call ya. Do I make myself clear?"

"Crystal!"

CHAPTER 10

I return to the station and take a seat behind what they call a desk. The one I had in third grade was bigger. But, being the new guy, I get the leftovers. They did throw in a filing cabinet, which is totally empty except for a package of snickers bars in the bottom drawer.

I normally don't get to sit in the office much. But since I have two death reports to write up, they have someone else out patrolling my area this morning.

I lean back in my chair with the notes of both incidents spread out before me. Now that we know what killed these two guys, we can eliminate the homicide theories – I think. The autopsy was quite revealing but I found myself now with more questions than answers. I just don't get it: A killer deer on the loose? If that's the case, then why did the second guy have two sets of holes in him?

I never really considered hunting as a dangerous sport, even while growing up. I do recall a time when my dad came home from a hunting trip in West Virginia back in the late 70's. I was about seventeen I guess, and still to this day, I remember the look of horror on his face.

The year was 1979. My dad, along with two hunting buddies (Doc and John), had made plans to hunt whitetail deer in West Virginia. They were going to an area called Mount Storm Lake. The name of this place was right on. The trees only grew on one side up there because of the fierce winter winds. They had hunted there many times before and had taken quite a few deer.

On Thursday night right after Thanksgiving, they packed up Doc's camper and headed out. It took about four hours but they eventually arrived at the Lake. Once there, they had to negotiate some dirt roads and managed to set up camp in quick fashion.

They bow hunted the rest of the day Friday and all day Saturday; Sunday was goof-off day. The trio found themselves in between the end of bow season and the start of gun season on Monday. That afternoon, they took a walk and came across another campsite. They made their introductions to a number of other hunters and learned that the group was from Maryland. Nice bunch of guys; just regular folks like themselves.

Monday morning finally came and the first day of buck season was in full swing. They all scouted the area during the bow season and had their hunting spots already picked out. Dad settled on a spot that had been logged out several years earlier.

It was about 9:30 in the morning when dad heard a shot above him. He picked up his rifle and watched intently. All-of-a-sudden he saw a deer with a large rack running through the timber. The deer was really spooked and making no future plans to slow down for a broadside shot. Dad tried everything to get a bead on him in the scope and finally, out of desperation, squeezed off a round. His shot didn't connect but it did cause the deer to change directions. Now the animal was running in a more open area where dad could at least get the scope on him. He fired several more times but couldn't seem to get a bullet to make contact. He eventually swung his rifle ahead of the deer for another open spot and fired one final time. This one made contact, sending the deer to the ground. Dad ran over to the buck and found one bullet hole right through the chest. My dad was so proud of his shot, but a little disappointed in himself that it took so many rounds to finally get him on the ground. One does tend to get excited in the heat of the moment. After field dressing the buck, he dragged it down to the truck.

Later that day, his hunting partners returned to the truck empty-handed. In West Virginia, you're allowed to buy a second buck tag and they had such a tag in their possession. Dad decided to hunt on the second day as well but at another spot.

Tuesday morning came quick, and the group parked the truck at the same spot as the day before. Dad walked a little farther up the mountain above the clear-cut area, making no plans to hunt real hard today since he already had a nice rack buck already hanging up back at camp.

It was about eleven o'clock when dad heard a shot in front of him that was close. He got his gun ready but didn't see anything at first. About fifteen minutes went by before seeing a hunter wearing fluorescent orange, running up the trail. He then saw several more hunters running down the trail to the area where he had heard the shot. Based on what he was seeing, he made the assumption that some hunters from the other camp were preparing to put on a drive. Dad decided to leave his spot due to the recent influx of human activity.

He walked down the trail to the dirt road and soon ran into another hunter who told him that someone had been shot but he didn't know who it was. Dad began to panic a little. All he could think about was his hunting partners and if they were okay. As he hustled down the road, he soon found his truck missing. Then the panic really set in.

As he approached the parking spot, he observed several hunters standing beside the camper where the Maryland hunters were staying. It was then that he saw a hunter lying on the ground close by. As dad drew closer, he saw no one rendering any assistance to the wounded man who he thankfully did not recognize. The guy took a direct hit from a 30-caliber round to his left side of his rib cage. He didn't appear to be conscious. He could see his heart beating inside the guys' chest and couldn't think of a thing that he could do for him. Dad said it took about ten minutes before the wounded man started to quiver and eventually die. He didn't need a doctor to tell him what he just witnessed. Several minutes later, dad's friend John showed up in the truck and announced that the ambulance was right behind him. But it was too late. Everyone just stood around in a state of shock.

What they later found out was that this guy had killed a deer on the first morning and left it in the woods. The next day, he went to retrieve it. The guy (for whatever reason) didn't put on his fluorescent orange suit and got more stupid by deciding to carry the deer out on his shoulders through the clear cuts. A local West Virginia hunter saw, what he thought was a nice buck walking through the clear cut, and fired. To his surprise, he had shot another hunter.

After the State Police and Game Commission people were on the scene, the group made a unanimous decision to return to Pennsylvania, never to return to this place ever again.

Dad arrived home with a nice eight-point buck; one that any hunter would be proud of. But his trophy buck lost its splendor due to the horror that played out in the woods that day. Dad had the deer mounted and to this day, it still hangs on the wall along with his other trophies. The buck has been a constant reminder of that day and how fragile life can be.

The rules established for hunting are there for a reason. This hunter decided not to follow those rules and died as a result. My dad became much more safety conscious as a result of what he witnessed. He reminded both my brother and me whenever we were in possession of any firearms.

I retrieve a report form from a stack I keep on top of my filing cabinet. Being the new guy I still don't have a computer to use. I sometimes get the feeling that Hanson pulled more than a few strings to get me in here. I get the impression they were not expecting my arrival when I was hired. That's nothing a little seniority wouldn't cure.

I begin filling out the form with name, address, and all the other preliminary information. I stop at line five where it asked for the information of the complainant; the person(s) who called this in.

It then dawns on me that no one at either scene came forward to claim they found the bodies. In all my years of police work, I have found that honest folks usually can't wait to come forward and tell their story.

I immediately call dispatch and Mandi answers.

"Hey girl."

"Hey babe. Why are you in the station?"

"I have to complete these death reports. I guess they consider this a priority today."

"Well I would guess so. According to everyone around here, this has never happened in these parts."

"Hey, I need you to do something for me. Pull the call sheets and get me the names and numbers of the persons who called in these two complaints."

"I've got them right here, Marvin. Just give me a second and I'll tell you.

After a few seconds of silence, Mandi comes back on the line.

"Hey Marvin, you're not going to believe this but both calls were anonymous."

"Anonymous!"

"Yeah. According to the entry on the sheet, the caller was a male who just gave the location of the body and hung up!"

"Did the 911 operator record the incoming phone number off the screen?"

"The call didn't come in through 911. It came in on the regular lines. Do you want me to pull the phone records and get you a number?"

"Would you?

"Only if you agree to finish what you started the other night."

"That was not my fault Mandi and you know it."

"I know – work first and me second."

"I don't have time for this, girl. We'll talk about this later. How long will it take for you to get the numbers?"

"I'll have them by the end of the day. I'll bring them over tonight after work."

"Sounds good. I'll see ya later."

I hang up and lean back once again. I find it hard to believe that out of two deaths, we don't have one person who can be questioned as to what they saw. I only ever came across this one other time. Back in my police days in Florida, I was investigating a complaint and the caller was anonymous. After a few weeks, we discovered that the caller was actually the perpetrator of the crime. Could this be the case? Could our perpetrator deliberately call so we would find the bodies? Do we have a perpetrator at all, or a mad deer running around sticking folks while they hunt? I know this investigation belongs to Gates and I should keep my nose out of it. But I don't think I'll do that. I feel connected in some way – but not sure how right now. Weird!

CHAPTER 11

I arrive at my apartment a few minutes before four. Nice easy day at work for a change. I was able to finish up my two death reports and get off work at my scheduled time, a rare event for this line of work. Mandi gets off at the same time but I didn't run into her when I left. I'm surprised that she's not here yet. She's got kind of a lead foot and always beats me to wherever. She is constantly accusing me of driving like a grandpa. As I get older, I just find myself no longer in a hurry to get anywhere. Not too fond of paying that one hundred dollar speeding ticket, either.

I enter my apartment and immediately head for the fridge. All I had to eat today was a Snicker's bar and a mountain dew from the vending machine. I normally don't eat so poorly, but with all that has been going on around here, I completely forgot to pack a lunch this morning. That normally wouldn't have been a problem but I forgot my wallet as well. I guess I could have bummed a few dollars from Mandi but I got so involved in those reports, it was two o'clock before I knew it.

I open the refrigerator door and locate a slab of pizza from the other night. Mandi was nice enough to wrap it up before it went bad.

I remove the foil and pop it in the microwave for forty-five seconds. Before the dinger dings, the door opens and Mandi burst in.

"Marvin – you're not going to believe this?"

"What!"

Mandi slams the door behind her.

"I researched both calls that came in on those deaths and I got a recording on cassette for you. And get this – both calls came in from the same number."

"Shut the hell up!"

"I'm serious. But that's not the half of it. I did a reverse search on the number and it comes back to a payphone right here in Bedford."

"Where in Bedford?"

"I don't know. But I do know there are only five payphones left in this town and the police stopped maintaining the records on these years ago when cell phones became so popular."

"So the people who called in were nowhere near the scene. Mandi, this is starting to get creepy."

"I know. I am beginning to see murder here Marvin and it's scaring the crap out of me."

"Do you know where the phones are in town so we can check them out?"

"I have a good idea where three of them are. But before we do that, you have to listen to these calls."

"Why?"

"Because I already did. Tell me what you hear."

Mandi pulls out a small cassette player from her coat pocket and slips the cassette inside the device.

"Where'd you get that?"

"I borrowed it from the station. They won't miss it for one evening."

She hits the play button and the first voice I hear is that of one of the dispatchers:

"Pennsylvania Game Commission"

"Yes ma'am, I'm calling to report the body of a dead hunter on Martin's Hill Mountain about a hundred fifty yards off Johnson Trail, right at the first bend near the cliffs."

"Okay sir, can I get your name please?"

A click is audible on the tape and nothing more is said by the man.

"Sir, are you there? Sir?"

The voice was that of a man – I think. The sound was somewhat muffled. But whoever it is, was not willing to wait around for their personal information to be recorded. I then listen to the second recording. I listen as the same voice from the same person recites the same words as before, except for the location of the body. I hit the stop button on the player.

"Marvin, what are we going to do?"

"Grab your keys; we're taking a ride."

CHAPTER 12

Mandi and I soon find ourselves heading down Oak Boulevard in her gray Ford Focus. I could have driven the Jeep but with the light bar on top and all of those decals, it has a tendency to attract attention. I don't want that right now. I'm looking into something I shouldn't be looking into. By department policy, I am required to call my findings into the lead investigator. And since Gates is the only investigator I know of, and I don't like him, I'll just do this myself.

But he may already know about this. If he doesn't, he should. He's been on the job for decades for Pete's sake. I figured this out in a few hours while doing a stupid death report with a little help from Mandi. Okay, a lot of help from Mandi.

We reach Wisdom Avenue and make a left turn.

"Where are we heading, girl."

"I know there's a payphone at this McDonald's up ahead. We'll check that one out first. If that's not the one, there's a Taco Bell on Dean that has a payphone as well."

"You really know your payphones."

"You're just saying that so you can get in my pants"

"Not really, but if that what it takes. Hey listen, did Gates or anyone else request copies of the incoming calls?"

"Not that I know of. In fact, I'm sure they didn't. We have to maintain a log in the back by the recorder for court purposes. When I saw the log, there were no entries for these. Why?"

"Just curious."

We arrive at the McDonald's and find a payphone just outside the main entrance. I have the number from the recordings jotted down on an old cable bill that I'll eventually have to pay if I want to continue to watch my Nascar races on Sunday afternoons.

I run up to the phone. The number I have written is 249-1450. The number on the phone displays 249-1458. I look over at Mandi who is still waiting in the car.

"This isn't the one."

I hop back into her Focus and we speed down Wisdom Avenue a few blocks and turn left again onto Dean Drive. I look ahead and see the lighted Taco Bell sign just above the tree line. In a few seconds, we are in the parking lot. This payphone is not attached to the building like the other one.

"Where is this one, Mandi?"

"I'm not sure. Oh, there it is, near the drive-thru."

Attached to a metal pole about ten feet from the drive-thru display is another payphone. Mandi parks in the adjacent lot next to a cigarette shop. With the suspect number committed to memory, I exit and approach the phone. With much anticipation I read off the numbers and a match is made.

"This is it, Mandi."

My first instinct was to pick up the receiver and call Hanson with my big new discovery. But the cop in me takes over and I remember the one thing that catches thousands of bad guys each year – fingerprints.

I run back to the car with Mandi still sitting behind the wheel.

"Let me use your cell phone. I left mine back at the apartment."

She hands me her slick new pink Sanyo that I wouldn't be caught dead using, and dial Hanson's number.

"Hello"

"Hey Hanson, are you busy?"

"I'm in the middle of dinner. What do you want?"

"I found out where the calls came in on the two deaths."

"So, big deal."

"It is a big deal! Let me clue you in on something. Both calls came from a payphone at the Taco Bell here on Dean Drive and both calls were made by the same person."

An eerie uncomfortable silence comes over the line.

"Hanson, did you hear that?"

"Yeah I heard ya. But how would anyone know about the two deaths in the mountains twenty miles away and know their exact location, unless…"

"Yeah, unless the caller is the killer."

"But Marvin, those guys were gord to death."

"I know, but who says a deer did it."

"Marvin, you better never let Gates know how good you are or he'll run you out of this town."

"Speaking of Gates, we need to get him down here and process this phone. From what I can tell, this thing doesn't get a lot of use. We may be able to get some prints off of this thing."

"I agree. You stay there and I'll get a hold of Gates and have him respond. I'll brief him on what you found so you two don't have to spend a lot of time together."

"I love you, man. I'll be here waiting."

CHAPTER 13

It's been a quiet week since the bodies were found. I've spent my shifts patrolling the back roads of this mountain checking hunting licenses and writing a few tickets for those who choose not to follow the rules of this game.

They processed the prints from the payphone but I've heard nothing as a result. And since we have no suspects or any evidence that we even have a suspect, who would you compare them to?

On Wednesday of this week, our department set up the robotic decoy. This is a life-like model of a whitetail deer that is equipped with a control box, which can move an ear or turn the deer's head with the flick of a switch. We use him periodically to lure unethical hunters who decide they would rather ride around the back roads and hunt from the comfort of their truck seat instead of doing it like it's supposed to be done.

We did the set up on Nike Road which is more of a two mile dirt lane the game commission carved out so hunters can get back to the deepest part of the woods. This relieved some of the congestion they were experiencing in the parking lots.

It only took about twenty minutes before an F350 came easing up the road. It was the passenger who first saw the decoy and called out to the other people in his hunting party. It's kind of comical to watch a hunter fling an arrow into the decoy and the thing doesn't go down or run off. This particular guy hit the deer three times before we reached him. He was so engrossed in the moment that when I tapped on his shoulder, he just about come out of his skin.

"Excuse me, sir: Officer Riggs with the Pennsylvania Game Commission."

"Can I help you, officer?" says the man with a confused look on his face.

"Yes you can. If you wouldn't mind, I'd appreciate it if you would stop plunking arrows into my decoy and put your hands behind your back."

We arrested a total of four people that morning for hunting from a roadway - a big no-no in this business. Those four individuals lost their vehicles, their equipment, and their hunting privileges for the next five years. I don't feel sorry for them though. They knew the rules, and that they apply to everyone. No one out here is privileged.

———

I'm back at the office now, finishing up some paperwork and looking forward to the next two days off. It's been quite a while since I have had this much time off. The department has been short a person up until last week. They brought a new guy in from New York. He's just a kid, about twenty four years old, and appears very eager to get started. They introduced him to me the other day and he seems nice. He possesses the standard Master's degree you need today in order to even breathe in this world.

I'm in the office early today for a reason. The second hunter we found was a married guy with a daughter. The wife is meeting me today at three-thirty so she can retrieve his person belongings, which we found at the scene.

It's going to be a rough time for her and I'll need to prepare for lots of tears and maybe a story or two. This is a task that Gates would normally handle, but he asked if I would do it. I guess he's busy doing whatever he does. I don't think this is any indication that our relationship is getting any better. He actually asked Hanson to ask me if I would do this. And you know how that goes. A request from a superior is basically an order.

After finishing up the daily log and other minor details, I retrieve a box from the bottom drawer of my filing cabinet. I chuckle to myself – finally, something is in here besides Snicker's bars.

The box has all the things the wife will be taking home with her this afternoon. I can picture her and her daughter later today going through things like his wallet, his watch, and both crying as they recall the memories of a good man who was their foundation for so many years. It is proof that no one ever leaves this earth. As long as someone out there is thinking of you, your existence is eternal.

As I lay the stuff out on my desk, a radio transmission goes out to Hanson from one of the dispatchers.

"214, just got a report of a signal seven on Martin's Hill."

A chill goes up my spine. A signal seven is the code for a dead body – another dead body. My first thought is this can't be happening. Three bodies found within a week of each other. I hope to God that this was some old geezer that maybe had a heart attack or something natural. But my gut feeling tells me otherwise.

"214 to 367."

"This is 367 go ahead Hanson."

"Is the new guy relieving you tonight?"

"10-4."

"When he gets there, have him respond to this call. You stay there and take care of that task I need you to complete."

"10-4"

—————————

The phone at my desk rings, which startles me. It's just not something I'm used to. The digital readout tells me its dispatch.

"Officer Riggs."

"Hey babe."

"Mandi you need to be careful with that."

"With what?"

"The babe stuff while we're working."

"Whatever. I'll call you babe whenever I want to."

"Okay, it's your job. What's up?"

"There's a Ms Santiago here in the lobby to see you. She's kind of good look'n. You got a new girl?"

"Hardly. She's the widow of one of the hunters we found."

"Which one?"

"The second guy we found. If you would, escort her back here for me. Boy, I'm sure not looking forward to this."

"I guess not. I'll be right there."

A few seconds slowly tick away as the sound of high-heeled shoes increases in volume as she and Mandi make their way to my desk.

"Ms Santiago?"

"Yes, and you are Officer Riggs?"

"Yes ma'am. Please have a seat."

We complete the customary limp handshake that most of us guys do whenever we are introduced to a woman. It's like we almost expect that all women are fragile and if we overpower them with a firm handshake, in some way we are being rude or something.

Mrs. Santiago immediately scans her late husband's belongings that

I have laying out on my desk. She reaches for his wallet and clutches it against her chest. As she does the tears begin to flow freely, as I find myself having to hold back my own.

"I am sorry for your loss ma'am. I do need you to make sure that everything is here and sign this property receipt after you're done."

"Okay" she says.

"Do you need some time alone?"

"No. I just want to get this done and get out of here."

"I understand."

As she slowly examines the watch and then the necklace like someone who's never seen these items before, she asks:

"Do you know who or what killed him yet?"

"We know what you know. He was impaled with a set of deer horns. If it was an accident or someone did this on purpose is still a mystery."

"He was a good man, officer. He loved to bow hunt. Said it was so relaxing to be out in the woods alone with his thoughts. It was a time for reflection for him. He always came home a nicer person than when he left."

"I understand ma'am. When I used to hunt, I always felt the same way. There is just something about being out there that can regenerate a person so they can take on the nasty and greedy world we live in."

"My husband used to say the same thing. You know, there is something missing."

"What's that?"

"A few years ago my husband purchased one of those digital cameras that you strap to a tree. They're mostly used for tracking deer. He liked using it to record himself hunting. I remember him bringing those pictures home and showing me them on the computer. Did you find a camera?"

"No ma'am. No camera."

"I know he took it with him. He always did."

"I'll check on that for you and if we find it, I'll give you a call."

"Thank you for your time."

I stand and see the fresh new widow to the door. She has what she came for – almost. I wonder what life will be like for her now.

As soon as the woman starts down the hallway, I can't help but wonder how conceited her late husband must have been. I never heard of anyone filming themselves hunting. That would make for a lot of boring video since ninety-nine percent of the time you just sit, and one percent of the time you're being killed.

"HOLY SHIT!!!"

I run to the phone and call Hanson's cell.

"Sergeant Hanson?"

"Meet me on top of Martin's Hill in about thirty minutes?"

"Why?"

CHAPTER 14

It's four o'clock in the afternoon when I arrive at the top of the mountain and our rendezvous point. Hanson is sitting at the trail waiting for me.

"Marvin, what took so long?"

"What do you mean? I got here in less than thirty minutes."

"So what's up?"

"We need to head down to where they found the second victim."

"The Mexican guy?"

"Yeah. You are not going to believe this but according to his widow I just spoke to, he never hunted without one of those digital cameras they use to scout for deer. I guess this guy really liked watching himself hunt."

"You mean we may have actual pictures of him being killed?"

"That's why we're up here Mark."

"HOLY SHIT!!!"

"That's what I said too."

"You know you're off the clock, right Marvin?"

"This one's on the house."

We start down Johnson Trail on foot with Hanson leading the way, following the rut marks from the vehicles investigating the third body.

"Where did they find the third guy?"

"They found this one on the right side of the trail down in the ravine that parallels the cliffs."

"It's thick as hell in there."

"Yeah. I don't know how they find him in all that."

"I bet I know. I bet someone twenty miles away called it in."

"Gates will handle that part. Remember Marvin, you're a patrolman – nothing more."

"You make me sound so useless."

"You know what I mean smartass. Just work real hard and when you grow up, you can be an investigator too, just like Gates."

"Now there's something to look forward to. I've always wanted to be overweight, crabby, and a royal pain in the ass with everyone I meet."

After about twenty minutes of walking, we arrive at the scene of the second victim. Almost all of the evidence that a murder took place here has been erased. All that is left is a reflective marker nailed to the very tree where Mr. Santiago met his death.

I immediately take a seat in the exact spot our victim was found in. I begin to scan the area in front of me looking for a needle in a haystack. It takes less than a minute to find it. There; just to the left of where Hanson is standing, about thirty yards out.

"There it is" I announce to whoever is listening.

I walk smartly to a young oak tree as Hanson speechlessly watches my every move. I arrive within seconds and stand before a device that most homicide detectives can only dream about; better known as the smoking gun; the nail in the coffin; the bada-bing. An outdoor digital camera securely fastened to a tree by way of a black nylon Velcro strap; and it's aimed directly at where our victim was found.

"Holy shit Marvin. I don't believe it."

"Neither do I. How do you miss that?"

"I have no idea"

"Do you suppose this guys entire death is on here."

"I sure hope so. And what was that comment you made earlier about growing up?"

"I take it back. Let's get Gates over here to process this."

CHAPTER 15

It's the next day and I find myself opening a door that I've never opened before. It's a room located in the very back of the station. Patrolmen are not privy to this drab eight-by-eight enclosure. It hosts only a desk and two chairs. No pictures, no plants, no filing cabinets, no nothing. It's the interrogation room.

As I make my entrance, I see Hanson holding up the one wall while Gates is sliding out a chair for me.

"Have a seat Mr. Riggs." Gates says.

"What's going on here?" I ask.

Hanson lets go of the wall and eases over while staring at me with a suspicious eye.

"Just sit down Marvin. You'll find out soon enough."

"Found out what?"

"SIT DOWN MR. RIGGS!"

Hanson has never called me by my last name with such an authoritative tone of voice. It sends chills down my spine just to here him say it. I do what he says out of fear – not compliance. He eases even closer.

"Give me your service weapon Marvin."

"NO!"

"SURRENDER YOUR WEAPON MARVIN OR YOUR EMPLOYMENT WITH THIS AGENCY IS FINISHED."

"What the hell is going on here?"

Mr. Gates decides to get involved in the discussion.

"Once we have your weapon, you'll know everything in a few minutes."

I reach down and unfasten the holster that secures my weapon. I remove it while Gates has his hand out to retrieve it. I immediately turn to Hanson and hand the weapon to him. Gates puts on his angry mask, which is just the reaction I want. He has done nothing but put me down since I got here. At least Hanson has been a friend – up until now.

"Okay: you have my gun. Now start talking."

Gates takes a seat in the only other chair available on the other side of the desk. Hanson resumes holding up the west wall. Gates reaches down between his legs and opens a briefcase. He retrieves a green folder and places in on the desk in front of me.

"Mr. Riggs. I wonder if you could tell me where you were at on the morning of October 1st of this year."

"Well that's easy. I was working. It was the first day of bow season. My shift started at six in the morning. Why?"

"I'll be asking the questions here."

"The hell you will. I've got some questions too."

"Mr. Riggs; before we go any further. I'll need to read you your rights."

"MY RIGHTS!"

"You have the right to remain silent. If you give up that...."

"I KNOW MY GOD DAMN RIGHTS SO DON'T BOTHER."

I turn to Hanson.

"Mark – do I need to get an attorney here?"

"Did you do anything wrong?"

"I've done lots of things wrong – but never illegal."

"Then you have nothing to worry about, so answer the man's questions."

I turn back to face Gates.

"I know my rights and I waive them. So what's going on?"

Gates reaches over and opens the folder. I watch as he removes a larger-than-normal colored photograph and turns it so I don't have to look at it upside down. I lean over the desk to get a good angle. The lighting in this room is for shit. The photograph is somewhat grainy but clear enough that you definitely see what's transpiring.

"Recognize anything in this picture Marvin?" ask Gates.

I do recognize the image captured. It's a photograph of the second victim in the woods. The picture shows him in a sitting position, just like we found him that afternoon. But I don't recognize the man standing over him wearing all camouflage, with blood dripping from a set of deer antlers he's holding in his right hand.

I lean back in my chair for a moment.

"This picture is from the camera we found, isn't it?

"Yes it is Marvin" Gates acknowledges.

"So I guess we don't have a mad deer running around thank God."

I refocus on the photograph. We have a mad man on the loose and his method of assassination is to say the least – odd. Why would someone go to these lengths? If you want to kill someone, just put a bullet in them. This is somewhat like a stage production. I lean forward again and address Gates.

"Who is this guy?" I ask. "The one holding the horns."

I turn the picture around and point to the unknown man in the photo so Gates can see what I'm referring to.

"Mr. Riggs; we were hoping you could tell us who that is."

"I don't have any idea who it is but I sure know how you could find out."

"How's that?"

"Whoever it is, has his hunting license pinned to his back. Run the damn number through the system."

"We did that Marvin."

"Well I would hope. So why are you talking to me?"

"Because Mr. Riggs; the license comes back to you."

"ME! That's impossible. I was working the morning this happened."

"We know Marvin," says Hanson. "We've already been over you're your log with a fine tooth comb along with your radio transmissions and the mileage on your vehicle."

"And so we're good – right?"

"The coroner says the man's death occurred between seven and nine o'clock that morning. From what we can tell, you were at the station during that time."

"Damn right I was."

Gates chimes in:

"Where is your hunting suit right now?"

"It's in my bedroom closet at the apartment. I haven't taken it out this year. I saw it just last week when I was grabbing for a dress shirt. I'll go get it if you want?"

"That won't be necessary. Our search team will find it."

"What search team?"

Gates reaches inside his vest pocket and pulls out a folded sheet of paper and tosses it in front of me

"What's this?"

"It's a search warrant. Our team is inside your apartment as we speak."

"This is just great! Now my landlord is going to see this and I'll have to find another place to live. Tell me you didn't sledgehammer the door?"

"That's up to the search team Mr. Riggs."

I knew from my patrol days what they do to front doors. Cops have this dislike for closed doors; especially when they have a search warrant in their pocket. The whole purpose of a search warrant is to gather evidence. And if you don't want your suspects flushing the evidence down the toilet, you have to go in fast and hard. But the evidence they are looking for is a hunting coat. There's no way that's going down any toilet I've ever seen.

All the talking in this room has stopped. I'm starting to get a little scared. No – I'm getting a lot scared. This whole thing is absolutely unbelievable. Someone is setting me up, but who? I know I don't have a lot of friends but I have even fewer enemies. The only person who doesn't really care for me around here is the guy sitting across from me. Could Gates mastermind this whole thing to get me out of here? I don't know but I'm sure as hell going to find out.

The silence in the room is broken by a radio transmission directed toward Gates. He picks up his two-way:

"214 go ahead."

"Be advised, no hunting suit here."

"Gates – tell them to look inside my bedroom closet. It's all the way in the back on the left."

Gates keys-up the radio again:

"Be advised, I have Mr. Riggs with me and he says to look inside the bedroom closet – all the way in the back to the left."

"10-4, we are standing inside the closet right now. No hunting suit."

"10-4"

"Guys – I'm telling you, it was in there a week ago. I saw it with my own two eyes."

"Who has access to your apartment?" asks Hanson.

"The only person is Mandi but she wouldn't have taken it. She has no reason to. Someone must have broken in and taken it. It's the only explanation I can come up with."

The room goes silent once again. Everyone staring at one another trying to figure out what the next course of action is going to be. It is obvious that Gates and Hanson did not come in here with a plan. I guess they were hoping I would jump up, admit my guilt, and walk myself over to the jailhouse. Not happening. I didn't do this but it's obvious someone out there wants the world to think I did.

"So what now gentlemen?"

Hanson shuffles over to the desk and squats down between me and Gates.

"We're going to put you on administrative leave with pay until further notice. It will give us some time to figure out what is going on here. I'll also need your badge before you leave."

"What about the press?" I ask.

"This entire investigation will be conducted with the absolute secrecy in order to protect you. Marvin, I'll be honest with you; I truly believe you had nothing to do with this and someone out there is setting you up big time. Stay as low and out of sight as possible until we find out who."

"Alright."

I stand and reluctantly remove the requested hardware. It's a difficult thing to do. Once you pin a badge on your chest, it becomes a part of you. Removing it can cause some anxiety disorder for sure. My hand shakes as I surrender it.

"It'll be okay Marvin" Hanson says.

The words embrace me.

CHAPTER 16

It's been two hours since the interrogation – my interrogation. It's no picnic being falsely accused of something no matter what it is. But we're not talking about stealing candy bars from the local store or knocking-up the neighbor girl here. We're talking about murder – three counts. We're talking about death penalty shit here. I'm not going down like this. No way. I've gotta find out who's behind this - and fast.

I make the left into dad's driveway. You can't see the house from the road and that's what we like. Remember; my dad is dead and we aim to keep him that way.

The driveway winds through the woods about a quarter of a mile. When he secretly built this place back here, he was doing the work himself. The bends in the road were made at the will of the smallest trees. Some of those one hundred year old oaks are a little much for one person; especially when you're pushing seventy.

I reach the cabin and park my Suzuki behind a pile of firewood. I don't bring the patrol vehicle back here. The last thing I need is for one of the other officers to see me driving back here and start asking questions.

I exit my car with a bag of groceries in hand. I come to visit about ever other week. Today's trip though is not for him - it's for me. Since my mom lives a thousand miles away in Florida, my dad is going to have to listen to me whine for awhile.

As I approach the front door, I'm startled by something I see hanging on a hook just to the right of the living room window: A hanging basket of flowers.

My dad bought a basket of flowers?

This is so out of character for him that it sent a chill down my spine. Something is up and I wish I knew what. I had no idea I was about to find out so quickly.

I arrive at the front door and knock as I always do. But this time was different. I didn't hear the usual "COME IN" from the back patio where he usually sits working on a gin and tonic. This time I hear tiny footsteps coming my way and they're moving quickly. The knob turns and the door swings open to reveal a woman standing inside.

"Hello" she says. Can I help you?"

Standing at the doorway is a woman I do not recognize. A Japanese lady in her late 40's who is well-dressed and happy to be alive.

"Hello; and who you are?"

"My name Cindy. Who you be?"

"I'm Marvin. Would there be a Chuck Riggins still living here, I hope?"

"Oh Chuck in back. You come in?"

"That would be nice, thank you."

The petite lady escorts me through the living room and toward the back patio, as the question about the flowers is answered. As I look around, I start to notice knick-knacks appearing everywhere. I quickly realize that this lady is not a visitor; she's moved in. I enter the back patio and my dad is in his easy chair catching an episode on the Discovery channel. I announce my presence to get his attention.

"Hey Marvin: Good to see you."

"You too old man."

I reach over and kill the sound on the TV, which is met with a look of disgust from the once head of household.

"You mind telling me who the lady is?"

"That's Cindy."

"Okay. And Cindy is…"

"Cindy is my girlfriend."

"Girlfriend?"

"Girlfriend."

"And she's living here?"

"All day long boy. You gotta problem with that?"

"Ah Yeah. Maybe you forgot about the shop thing and the fact that you're up here because the world thinks you're dead."

"Boy; I've been up here now for two years and I'm starting to go stir crazy. I sit out on this back patio and talk to people who aren't there."

"Does she know?"

"Not really."

"Explain not really."

"I told her that I'm up here on the witness protection program and my location has to remain a secret."

"Oh, that's just great. So when you piss her off, she can run to the authorities and tell them all about you. And then when they find out that you're among the living, they'll find out that I knew about it, and I'm standing on the unemployment line."

"It'll be fine Marvin. Thanks for bringing the groceries. I appreciate it. So what's new with those hunters they found on your mountain?"

"If you can keep it to yourself, I'll tell ya. You can't even say anything to your new girl there."

"Her name is Cindy."

"Yeah whatever. Still not crazy about her being here. And where did you meet her? You know what, don't tell me: I don't even wanna know."

I tell dad about the false accusations being thrown at me and how he'll be seeing more of me now that I'm on an indefinite vacation. Dad is good to not interrupt as I tell my side of the story. He waits until I am finished to comment.

"Who did you piss off?"

"Man I wish I knew. I can't help but think it has something to do with you. You don't think maybe one of them are after me for little payback do ya?"

"It wouldn't make any sense to do it now, Dad say. You were in Wisconsin for two years prior to coming up here. If they wanted you, they'd a got you then."

"Yeah I guess. And who is left. The woman in the woods is dead, her husband Raymond was killed in that so-called car accident. We know Leroy was killed out on the highway, and you took care of Blue. So who else could there be?"

"You got me Marvin. Sounds like you better hide out too. Before you know it, you'll have a lady moving in with you."

"That won't be happening any time soon. Don't think Mandi would appreciate that. Besides, if you think I'm going to sit around and let someone else determine my fate – not happening. I've got an idea who might be behind this."

I make the left out of my dad's pothole riddled driveway with the intent on going home. All of this craziness is starting to wear me down a bit. I feel like I'm being watched; like they're out there patiently waiting for me to screw up so they can pounce and put some closure on this case.

My drive back to the apartment will be about a twenty minute ride. I have no deadlines to meet today so I can take my time. I reach up and hit the on button to my radio. You don't get many stations up here so my radio dial is preset to 101.2 which plays mostly 80s rock and roll. Still can't shake my addiction for those screaming guitars. But just as the Scorpions finish rocking me like a hurricane, the DJ immediately goes into the news with a special report.

"An update for those of you who are following the story of the dead hunters found on Martin's Hill Mountain: Sources close to the investigation have reported that a suspect is being questioned in connection with those deaths. Word has it that an Officer Marvin Riggs with the Pennsylvania Game Commission is a person of interest in those deaths. No charges have been filed at this time. Stay tuned to 101.2 for the latest on this case."

Before the DJ can even finish his story, I've got my cell phone out and speed dial Hanson. My heart races as I wait for an answer.

"Hello."

"HANSON. THANKS A LOT FOR KEEPING THE INVESTIGATION QUIET."

"Marvin, calm down. What's up?"

I pause to collect myself as to not sound hysterical.

"I just heard the DJ on the radio tell the whole freak'n world that I was hauled in for questioning."

"Marvin, that's impossible. No one knows about this except for those in that room. I know for a fact that nothing has been said outside those walls."

"Well someone said something because it's all over the damn radio. They mentioned me by name and that I'm a person of interest. It's got to be Gates. I'm sure of it. He hates me and will stop at nothing to see me out of here; even if it means prison."

"Marvin. I have known Gates for quite some time and his bark is worse than his bite. Let me call the radio station and find out where they got their information. Keep your cell handy. I'll be calling right back."

The line goes dead but my heart continues to race.

"Bullshit" I say out loud. "This is absolute bullshit."

Slamming my fist repeatedly against the defenseless dashboard, I know now what it must have been like for that guy in "The Fugitive" movie who is falsely accused of killing his wife. The inner struggle to remain calm competing with mustering the inner strength to prove yourself innocent is physically draining. And all the while: no one listening. There's just one difference thou: they will listen to me – I can assure you of that.

I down shift and hit the left turn signal, as I've done for the past couple of months in preparation to turn into my apartment complex. My hope is to escape from the world for a few hours until I can come up with a plan to counter this mess I find myself in. Gates is on my mind. He has to be the one who is behind this. But how does one investigate an investigator. I assure myself that if anyone can do this, I can.

As I look to my left and start my turn, I see something that doesn't look quite right. The parking lot has more vehicles in it than I've ever seen before in the middle of the day. Usually folks are at work and since there is no bus service here in town, they take their cars with them. I then catch sight of a white van parked directly in front of my apartment. The logo on the side reads: Channel 12 News.

I immediately ignore my turn and proceed down the two-lane road. I know what I just saw and why I just saw it. They're here to interview me. They want answers to questions I don't have. Of course they too listen to the radio and in a town where a possum can get front-page coverage for getting splattered on the roadway, I'm sure they are looking for a story with aspirations of being interviewed for the next opening on meet the press.

I quickly look over again as I make my escape and see well-dressed women with microphones waiting for my arrival. Each diva has a gentleman with them holding cameras the size of bazookas.

I reach for my cell and dial the station.

"Pennsylvania Game Commission."

"Mandi in dispatch please."

"Is this Marvin?"

"Yes Hazel, it is."

"You're all over the news. You seem like a nice guy."

"Hazel, don't believe everything you see on TV; now get me Mandi please."

"Without an acknowledgement, the line is transferred and Mandi comes on."

"Dispatch."

"Mandi"

"Marvin, you're all over the news. They say they have evidence that you killed these people."

"I didn't kill anyone. You know that. Listen; news vans are parked in front of my apartment. I need to go hideout somewhere. I'm heading over to your place. I just wanted you to know."

"Hey Marvin, I don't think that's a good idea."

"WHY?"

"Well; I think it would be best if you just stayed away for now. I can't lose my job and, well.."

"Well what? You don't trust me now?" You think I had something to do with this."

"I don't know what to think Marvin. Please don't go to my place – please."

"Unbelievable. Thanks Mandi. I really appreciate the support."

I disconnect the call and head out of town. Whatever happened to innocent before proven guilty? I guess that idea went out the window along with payphones and cassette tapes. Anymore, the mainstream media is so entrenched in our everyday lives that no one takes the time to stop and validate what is being reported. Everyone just assumes that whatever is being told to them is fact.

I head out of town in hopes of finding a place I can rest and get away from all of this. A few miles down the road, I see a sign for a Best Western. A motel room will do me just find today. Need some time to clear my head along with my good name. Isn't it ironic that I came up here to get away from the hustle and bustle of the big city? Go figure.

CHAPTER 17

Motel rooms are the loneliest places on earth; and a bit on the pricey side. Forty-five bucks to spend not even twenty-four hours. It's no wonder so many commit suicide in these places. Being stuck in a room such as this is just one step away from being homeless. But the solitude will do me good. I need some quality time to come up with a plan to combat whoever or whatever is out to get me.

My life up until a few years ago was pleasantly uneventful. Although I bitched and complained about it at the time, I would give anything right now to have that back. I always prided myself on being able to stay out of trouble.

I remember when I was a teenager about fifteen or so, my group of friends decided that it would be cool to start breaking into some cars around town and grab themselves some stereo equipment. They would start out as soon as the sun went down. I always found myself in the suspect vehicle for some reason. My friend Dave knew I was not crazy about what was going on and would always ask if I was cool with this. Not sure where it came from but that voice always told me not to get involved. That voice had an arm and would tap me on the shoulder whenever something was amiss.

I always told Dave I wasn't up to participating and the group always gave me the option to be dropped off somewhere, which I accepted without hesitation.

The crime spree lasted a few weeks until one evening; one of the perpetrators got busted. With a little police pressure, the names started flying and one by one each person that took part was hauled into the station. Of course, my name was mentioned, but in a different light. Everyone vouched that I did sometimes ride in the vehicle prior to the thefts but always left before and never took part. My friends stood up for me that day. I think deep down inside they were envious that I had the willpower to resist the peer pressure and walk tall down my own path.

My dad was present at the time and was quite proud of me. I remember when we got back from the station and he told my mom that I was the only one out of the bunch with a brain inside his head and had the ability to use it. It was one of the reasons I got a car at the age of sixteen. That incident convinced my dad that I was mature enough to handle a car at that age. It was only a few months later, after I got the car, that I wrecked the damn thing while out drinking with my friend Dave one evening. Yeah: So much for using my brain.

It's been a few hours since I checked-in and have done nothing but stare at the ceiling; brainstorming hundreds of ideas on how to retaliate and clear my name. I've come to a few conclusions. I will have to go outside to get anyone to help me. Now that my face is all over the news, I won't be able to enlist the help of anyone – not even Mandi it appears. I may have to come up with a disguise of some sort. I also know that whatever evidence I find to clear this injustice will be obtained illegally. I'll need to break some laws to get what I need.

My stomach is now reminding me that it's in need of some attention. The thought of calling for room service is quickly disregarded as I look over the menu and see the inflated prices. Eight dollars for a cheeseburger is a little out-of-hand. I don't care how hungry I am. I've always had the inner strength to resist such temptations. Whenever I see someone taking advantage of me (such as in the case of this cheeseburger rip-off), I never give in. It infuriates me that they think they have a captive audience, that they have me under a barrel so to speak.

After a few hours of watching daytime television and consuming a few cheeseburgers via room service, I am getting somewhat bored. As I reach for the channel changer for the one hundredth time, my cell rings. The number on the caller ID is one I don't recognize.

"Hello"

"Marvin, this is Gates. Where are you at?"

"I'm hiding."

"I figured that, but where?"

"You know Gates; I'm really not thrilled about giving out my location; especially to someone who I suspect is behind all of this."

"I may be an asshole from time to time but I can assure you, I don't have the energy anymore to go after people like you. Besides; believe it or not, I kind of like you. You're like me in a lot of ways."

"Oh, I can't wait to hear this comparison."

"It's true. You're a little on the rough side like myself, and you have a good eye for detail. I just don't like it when one of you guys come in and start showing me up. My ego has a tendency to bruise without much contact."

"So why are you calling me?"

"We need to talk."

"Okay, so talk."

"No. We need to meet somewhere. I want to show you something."

My gut reaction is to tell this guy to jump off a cliff. But I'm going to need help here. Even my girlfriend has abandoned me for the time being. But what if Gates is setting me up? What if they've decided to go ahead and arrest me? Hold me until they've got the evidence to prove they're case one way or the other.

"Okay, but Gates I swear, if you're setting me up, I'll hunt you down until my last dying breath. You hear me?"

"I hear ya. Do you know where Sporty's bar is at?"

"Yeah, it's out on Riser Road."

"Let's meet there around ten o'clock tonight."

"Okay but there's one problem. My mug has been on every television newscast all day. Everywhere I go, I'll be recognized. We will never be able to have a conversation. And if someone sees me talking to you, you'll be in some kind of trouble for consorting with the enemy so to speak."

"Yeah you're right. Why don't you put on some disguise?"

"I could shave off my mustache and goatee. I've got some hair dye back at the apartment I could use. I'm getting a little tired of this gray as it is. But my apartment is being staked out as we speak. A few hours ago, there were news vans parked in the parking lot just waiting on me."

"I can take care of that. In fact, I'm pulling into your complex right now. Wait thirty minutes and then head straight to your place. They'll be gone by then."

"What are you going to do Gates?"

"Well if they think your somewhere else, I'm sure they'll go to that location – wouldn't you?"

CHAPTER 18

I don't know what Gates told those news people but I do know when I got to my apartment thirty minutes later, there wasn't a soul in sight. Gave me the time I needed to get some of my personal stuff. I was able to load my car up with some clothes, my shaver, toothbrush, and that all-important hair dye.

It's now ten o'clock and I'm sitting in the parking lot of my vehicle at Sporty's. The lot is somewhat empty this evening and that's just fine with me. I enter through the back entrance and weave my way up to the bar. Sporting a new hair color of autumn brown that for some reason is starting to turn orange, I look around the room trying to find Gates. It doesn't take long to locate the fat guy sitting adjacent to the high-definition television catching an episode of Law and Order. Why do cops watch cop-shows? You'd think we get enough of this crap on a daily basis. But I always found myself trying to figure out who the bad guys was. I guess that is the allure of those shows. If you determine who the villain is before they reveal it, somehow you're smarter than they are. Cops are the most egotistical group of folks you'll ever meet. We always have to be better or smarter than everyone else.

I approach Gates who catches sight of me out of the corner of his eye.

"Hey Marvin, saved you a seat."

"Thanks Gates."

"Call me Roy."

"I'll stick with Gates until I figure out what you're up to."

"That's your choice. I almost didn't recognize you with your new orange hair dew."

"Yeah. I must have left it in too long. I got rid of the mustache and goatee too."

"I see that. I don't think anyone will recognize you for the time being."

"Good. So why are we meeting? And why are you being so friendly now?"

"Because I don't like it when innocent people are being railroaded."

"Okay, I'm listening."

"I don't know if you are aware but every autopsy is recorded via audio tape. And as a matter of practice I will occasionally listen to the autopsy report if I can't be present. I've been able to solve a few crimes in my years through comments or statements made by the medical examiners."

"Was the one I went to recorded?"

"Yes it was Marvin, which is why I called you here tonight. Prior to you getting there, the examiner withdrew a vile of blood from the victim. I know this because he said so while he was doing it. And I could hear Hanson in the background talking while this was being done. Just this afternoon, I pulled the autopsy report from the victim's file and the examiner mentioned the vile but I couldn't find any results."

"Well maybe the results aren't back yet."

"That's what I thought until I went to retrieve the vile from the storage locker. There is no vile Marvin – it's gone."

"Gone?"

"Yes, gone. No one has a record of it being drawn or logged in."

"Did you ask Hanson about it?"

"Marvin. You just don't lose something like that. That would be like misplacing the murder weapon. Hanson was the only other person in that room before you got there."

"So you're saying that Hanson might have something to do with setting me up?"

"Just think about it. He brings you all the way over here from Wisconsin. He gets you in the academy within weeks. I know guys who have been waiting a year to get into that school. You get assigned the very area that you requested."

"But he said there was an opening."

"There was no opening. They created a spot for you guy. Don't kid yourself. And what about keeping this thing quiet until they had time to investigate it further. Don't you find it odd that your mug was all over the news within an hour of you leaving that room?"

Gates was making sense – a lot of sense. More sense than I cared to hear. But Hanson was my friend, my confidant. Could this have been a set-up from the word go? Is he some sicko that needed a fall guy to carry out these murders?

"Okay, you got my attention. But I'm having a little trouble thinking Hanson would go through all of this to frame me. I can usually see through people and he just doesn't seem to be the type."

"I know - they never do."

"So what do you suggest I do?"

Gates reaches into his coat pocket, retrieves a small piece of paper, and hands it to me. I open the folded piece and observe a series of number.

"What's this?"

"It's the code to get into the medical examiner's office. Thought you might want to go after-hours and look around. Never know, you might find that missing vile of blood and have it analyzed yourself. You might find that those folks were drugged before they were killed."

"I don't get it Gates. Why don't you do it?" You're the lead investigator on this one."

"Not anymore. I was informed today by the big guy not to do anything else on this case."

"The chief told you that?"

"Yeap. You need to get out of here now. Keep your head low and your eyes open. There's a rat in the cellar and he's disguised to look like one of us."

"Thanks Roy. I appreciate it."

With a nod of his head, I quickly make my exit and get into my vehicle. Locking the doors behind me, I sit for a moment staring at a young couple in a car in front of me. There verbal argument is audible even over Toby Keith playing inside the bar. From what I can make out, the argument is over two hours last night he can't account for.

I head out of the parking lot with a load on my mind. Could it be that Hanson is setting me up? I just can't believe he, of all people, would go to these extremes to get me here in order to have a suspect for this crime spree. He could have found a homeless dude from downtown to do that. It just makes no sense.

CHAPTER 19

It now one o'clock in the morning and I'm preparing to do a little breaking and entering. With the building's security codes committed to memory, I hope there's not much breaking going on. There sure as hell will be some entering. Either way you look at it, it's a felony.

Prior to going home from the bar, I stopped by the apartment and loaded up my bicycle to use as my getting-away vehicle. I have this twenty-one speed Trek that is fast and quiet. Being an avid cyclist, I have found that one can sneak through the streets of a city at night virtually undetected. If I did need to make a quick escape, the odds of them chasing me through someone's back yard was unlikely.

I've even gone as far as to wear all black to avoid detection. I stare at myself in the mirror trying to get a handle on what I'm going to do if and when I get inside this place. I chuckle at my appearance. Every piece of clothing to include my shoes is black. I look like a middle-aged ninja preparing for a night of trick or treat.

With no plan at all, I head down Pelke Road, which runs parallel to the back of the motel. This is a back road into town consisting mostly of long driveways back to various farms. As I make my way through the winding countryside, I see lights way off in the distance from the farmhouses that occupy these hundred acre parcels. Most of the lights are from kerosene lanterns and not from electric. The folks who call this part of the world home are Amish. No electric, no gas, no cars, no modern conveniences what-so-ever. I have always been envies of these folks. They truly have it figured out. If I were Amish right now, I wouldn't be in the mess. And I certainly wouldn't be riding my five-hundred dollar bicycle through mounds of horse shit left on the roadway by the buggies they use for transportation. Some of which is being flung onto my back from the rear tire. Yeah; it's starting to offend.

I arrive at the medical examiner's office by one forty-five. Everything is going well – too well. I didn't see a car or person the entire way here. I park my bike in some bushes on the north side of the building. Before approaching the rear door, I take a moment to look around. No lights on inside and no cameras. Being that this is small town with a small town budget, security is not a top priority. This town only has two cops patrolling the streets that I know of. One for dayshift and one for the evening shift. I don't know what they do if one of them wants to take a vacation.

After a few minutes of making sure all is clear, I ease my way to the back door of the office. It's forty some degrees outside and I'm sweating like a French whore on dollar night. The fear of getting caught is taking over me. I guess this is what happens when you have a conscious. But I'm not here to commit a crime. I'm not about to enter this government building with the intent on stealing something or to do anyone any harm. I just want to prove my innocence – that's all. And since no one else seems to be interested in finding out the truth; it's up to me to take the lead.

I arrive at the door and find a punch-pad of numbers from zero to ten. With the code given to me by Gates, I begin punching in the six digit number. As I hit the last number, I can hear the locking mechanism deactivate. I wait a few seconds anticipating the alarm system to go off. It would be my luck. But all is quiet and I quickly enter and punch the same sequence of numbers on the alarm panel just inside the hallway, just like Gates had instructed me to.

I make my way down the hall and enter the autopsy room through the same door I went through a few days ago. The smell is even worse at night. Even with the temperature in the forties, the aroma of decaying flesh is nauseating. With a mini flashlight on my key ring, I scan the room, keeping the outer beam of the light down so that it's not visible from someone passing by.

I soon discover why the smell is so bad in here. A body is stretched out on one of the tables with a sheet covering most of the body cavity. It appears that someone forgot to put it away in one of the coolers or maybe they were halfway into the autopsy and the quitting time bell sounded. Either way, I can't help but aim the beam of my light over and see the face of a young woman who met with an untimely ending. Staring at death is not new to me so I am in no way startled by what I see. I find myself studying the face and not focusing on the task at hand. That'll sometimes happen whenever you recognize a corpse.

I stare at the face of the woman I confronted a few days ago in the parking lot at Martin's Hill; the same woman who was the HBIC (head bitch in charge) of the PETA brigade; the very same woman who I told the old guy Elmer to shoot if she or any of her followers tried to follow them. A new kind of fear now runs up my spine; the kind of fear where I could do prison time. But who am I kidding. I'm already in jeopardy of going to prison if I don't prove my innocence and quickly. I resist the urge to lift up the sheet and see if she was stuck with an arrow. I need to get down to business. I need to find that vile of blood.

I turn my flashlight off for now. My eyes are starting to adjust and I can now see the contents of this room from the small amount of light being generated from the two computer monitors left on overnight. I scan the room and see a small box that resembles a refrigerator sitting on the counter. Not a bad place to start looking for blood.

My law enforcement days taught me a great deal about this life-giving substance. I recall being assigned to bag up a bloody rag found at a homicide many years ago. Having been with the department for only a few weeks, I just assumed that any bag would do. So from the trunk of my patrol car I secured a black plastic baggie and soon placed the bloody rag inside. After sealing the bag with red evidence tape and completing the necessary paperwork to maintain a chain of custody, I drove to the station and dropped it into the evidence shoot next to the armory.

It was a few days later when I was called into the Sergeant's office and informed of an unhappy technician at the lab. I was sternly explained that blood and blood evidence has to be either chilled or allowed to breath to keep it from spoiling. My plastic baggie idea was a big no-no in this business and a ten minute tongue lashing made sure I never forgot it.

I arrive at the frig and wouldn't you know it; there's a pad lock on the damn thing. And not just one of those wimpy ones either. It was one of those locks that you see on TV where the guy shoots at it with a high-powered rifle and it still remains locked. I'll need to find a key.

I head out of the autopsy room and into an office next door, keeping my head down and my eyes constantly looking outside to make sure no one sees me in here. I'm also thanking my luck stars that I've been in this place before and have a good sense of where everything's at. I remember seeing the sign above the door that indicated this was

Winger's office. He's the head honcho around here so if anyone would have a key – it would be him.

I walk behind the desk and start pulling on drawers. To my surprise, they're all unlocked and ready for inspection. With the flashlight now securely held between my teeth, I begin going through the personal effects of one Dr. Joseph Winger.

I start with that long thin drawer directly underneath the desktop. A quick scan finds a small ring of keys sitting inside a small black tray. I secure the keys and continue my search. The thrill of going through other people's stuff overwhelms me.

You can tell a great deal about a person by their personal effects. I'm not sure why I feel the need to continue. My first impression of the doctor from last week's meeting gave me a sense of a family man with a few kids and a comfortable house just outside of town. As I begin to open drawers, the surreal picture of this man in my head is starting to cloud a bit. In the top drawer to my right, I find a .380 caliber pistol loaded to the brim with the required ammunition. Not something most folks keep nearby. I can only assume that he has it with him for protection with all the workplace violence going on these days. But wait, most of the people who come in here are dead to begin with. How threatening can that be?

I close the drawer without handling the gun. No need to leave any more evidence than I probably am. I look through the rest on the drawers on the right side and find nothing more than loose papers and a box of Ritz crackers half eaten.

I then proceed down the left side of the desk. The bottom drawer is packed with file folders that I figure are old autopsy reports from before the computer-age hit the big screen. I thumb through many tabs that protrude revealing the names of folks who are no longer with us. I half-heartedly look at the names until one jumps out and hits me square between the eyes.

"John Merrick"

The sight of this name sends me backwards. I fall on my ass, never taking my eyes off the tab.

"It can't be." I mutter under my breath.

Before me was the name of the man who was in my dad's workshop the night the assassins showed up. The same man who took two bullets to the back of his head for my father. The same man who died and is buried in the ground in Greencastle with a headstone that reads the name: Charlie Riggs.

With my adrenaline suddenly spiking to harmful levels, I snatch the file and immediately open it to see what I can find. Nothing; but a black and white photo of a man I do not recognize. Could this be the face of Merrick? I never saw his face, and I don't know anyone who has. There must be a hundred John Merrick's in this world. What are the chances? Without thinking too much about it, I place the photograph in my shirt pocket and return the folder. Not sure why but I don't have the time to analysis this one. John Merrick is dead and my father is safely hiding out in his cabin. I owe this man a lot but how to do repay a dead man. The answer is – you don't.

I shuffle back to the autopsy room with the set of keys in hand begin the task of opening the refrigerator. A few seconds later, I find myself staring at three rows of glass vials, each one individually named and numbered by someone with great penmanship. After looking at all twenty-seven vials, I'm convinced that the sample that I need is not here.

After ten more minutes of searching everything I am able to lawfully get into and finding nothing, I cut my losses and prepare to exit this place. I ease out the back door and make my escape as quickly as I had entered. I hop on the bike and begin the ride back to the motel. I hit the dark country road, feeling good that I was able to pull this off and not get caught in the process. With each thrust of the pedal, the name John Merrick keeps going through my head over and over again. Why is there a file in Winger's desk with this guys picture inside? Does he know something about my father? Does he have information about who is buried back home? Being who I am, I can't dismiss it. I need to learn more about Winger. That's all I need is to have another problem to deal with.

CHAPTER 20

My alarm clock is now reading six-thirty. I've been staring at it all morning, watching each minute click away. Probably good I'm suspended from work or I'd be of no use to anyone today.

I jump out of bed and find my cell phone. I am standing in front of the bedroom mirror staring at myself in my underwear impressed at my shape for being in my late forties. Most men my age haven't seen their feet in years. The only issue I have this morning is my orange hair.

I hit the number three on my cell phone and activate the speed dial for Hanson. The phone rings several times before I get a response.

"Hello"

"Hey Hanson, it's Marvin"

"Marvin? It's six-thirty in the morning."

"Yeah, I know. I need to talk to you."

"Now?"

"Yeah, now. Can I come over before you head to work?"

"I took the day off. I was planning on sleeping in and later take the kids out for lunch. Can't we talk on the phone?"

"No. I need to talk to you face to face."

"Marvin. I'm under strict orders to avoid any discussion with you about the homicides."

"You know Mark, someone is setting me up and if you think I'm going to just sit around and wait for them to fabricate a case against me, and go to jail for the rest of my life – it ain't happening. And another thing, I've been told by someone that I am not going to mention that you might be involved in framing me for these murders."

"Marvin – come on!"

"I know! You and I have been friends for quite awhile, and I would never think you would be the type that would do that to even your worst enemies."

"Come on over."

"Thanks. I'll be there in about an hour.

―――――――――――――

I pull into the driveway on my bicycle at Hanson's three bedroom ranch located on the outskirts of town. A simple house he built with his father a number of years ago when he got married. Hanson has a few acres in the back for his daughter to play in. Nice place and he takes good care of it.

I'm met at the front door by Hanson who has only managed to get a pair of pants on.

"Come on in Marvin."

"Thanks for the time. I won't take much of it."

I take a seat on the couch.

"Are you doing okay Marvin? You look like shit."

"Thanks. I didn't sleep at all last night. In fact, I can't remember last time I slept through the night. I guess it's that whole prison thing looming around me."

"How's Mandi doing?"

"She told me to stay away from her until this settles down."

"Sorry to hear that."

"I guess she doesn't want to be seen with me. Don't wanna give her a bad reputation."

"You know, it may just be that orange hair that is scaring her away. What the hell did you do?"

"It's my disguise. What do you think?"

"It's bad man – really bad. So what did you want to talk about?"

"Tell me what you know about Dr. Winger."

"The medical examiner guy?"

"Yeah"

"I don't know too much. He just got here about three months ago, right before you came on board. I don't even know where he came from. The other guy, Dr. Winegarden retired and they brought this guy in."

"Who brought him in?"

"Whoever hires medical examiners I guess. I would assume the chief had a big hand in it since most of the work they do is for the criminal justice side. Why are you asking?"

"Because something has been brought to my attention that doesn't add up, and no, I'm not going to tell you what it is."

"Marvin – you should really just stay out of this and let them find out who's responsible."

"Do you know what it's like Mark to be afraid to walk outside and be faced with a public who has already convicted you of something you had nothing to do with? I get stares from people who wouldn't believe. They point and sneer and whisper to their significant others 'There's the guy.' I can tell you, I'm a little sick of it."

"I guess I can't blame you. But you really need to let them do their job."

"You keep saying they – Why? Aren't you doing the investigation?"

"Not anymore. They took me off the case along with Gates. You didn't hear."

"No"

"Well you will. They called in two guys from the FBI. I can't believe they haven't contacted you yet."

"I guess if they saw me here, you'd be in some trouble."

"I'd have to answer some questions."

"Maybe I'd better go."

"Marvin – I'm on your side buddy. Don't forget that. I know you don't have the hate in you to do what someone did to those people up on that mountain. I guess I feel the same as Mandi does right now."

"I understand, Mark. Thanks for the little bit of info."

I quickly make my exit and head down the long driveway toward the main road. Not sure why I came. I guess I just needed to hear from Hanson himself that he was on my side. He says he is, but I keep going back to that old adage: Believe nothing you hear and only half of what you see. If only one could see lies.

CHAPTER 21

It's a chilly morning here in Bedford. I don't mind it though. There's nothing like a bike ride through the rolling hills of this area to wake a person up, along with these cool temps slapping you in the face. I need it too. I need to clear my head and decide what's next. I really don't have much to go on. I found a folder with John Merrick's name on it and a picture – big deal. Oh yeah, Dr. Winger has been here three months.

The thought of calling those FBI guys and setting up a polygraph test crosses my mind. But I've always been suspect of those tests. They don't work well when you're dealing with someone that has a conscience like mine.

I remember back many years ago, when I was working at a small convenience store in Florida, before my cop days. The store would undergo a monthly audit and inventory to make sure that the amount of money coming in, matched the merchandise going out. On this one particular audit, I guess things weren't adding up and I was ordered to take a polygraph. I remember asking if I had the right to refuse the test and was promptly advised that if I refused, I would be fired. Don't think they can do that anymore. We're talking a good twenty years ago.

So I went to a neighboring town and entered the office of a man with the whitest hair I ever saw. Prior to being strapped into the chair, we chat about what questions he would be asking me during the test. The one question was 'did I ever extend credit to anyone?' I remembered this one old lady who came in and bought an arm full of items but forgot her wallet. She was a sweet lady who was a regular customer of mine. I allowed her to take the items home and a few hours later, she came back to the store and paid for them. You would think I would be praised for my customer service skills. Wrong! Based on that omission, my employment was terminated the next day.

I pled my case but to no avail. This rinky-dink outfit found their scapegoat. So based on the fact that I extended a helping hand to a little old lady one day justified the audit and problem solved. So needless to say the word polygraph has left a bad taste in my mouth ever since. But if I have to in order to clear my name, I say strap me in and let's get those needles a-jumping.

The morning ride is turning out to be a good one. Just fifteen minutes and I'm already starting to work up a sweat. The perspiration against the cool morning temperature feels as good as a dip in a Jacuzzi on a cold winter night. As I proceed down one of the back roads toward my motel room, I decide that it's time to head back to my apartment. No more hiding from the enemy; that being the media and the rest of the public who has already convicted me in the court of public opinion.

I stop and check on traffic to my right, with the intent on proceeding north of Creek Road. Just then, I hear a car coming up behind me. I turn and witness a large black sedan approaching the intersection faster than I would like. As any safety-conscious rider would do, I wait for the sedan to arrive at the intersection with plans on letting them go and avoid any contact. I did not get my wish.

The sedan slams on the brakes and slides sideways directly in front of me. Before it even comes to a stop, the passenger's side rear door quickly swings open and a man in a three-piece suit exits. This guy is straight out of the one of the Godfather movies and approaches me with a purpose:

"Mr. Riggs?"

"Yeah, who are you?"

"There's someone that would like to have a word with you."

"Really. Tell them I'm not interested."

I turn and put my right foot on the pedal with the sole purpose of getting the hell out of here, but my plans suddenly change. The wannabe gangster reaches underneath his coat and pulls out a large caliber handgun and starts waving it in my direction.

"I said there's someone that would like to have a word with you."

I stop in my tracks. I stare at the man to get a sense of how serious he is. This man is serious – dead serious. He even has the hammer back on the pistol so that an easy squeeze of the trigger will do me away quickly. I suddenly have the urge to chat.

The man motions for me to enter the vehicle. I step forward and my bike falls into the ditch. I enter the vehicle from the rear door and sit beside a man who looks more gangster than the other guy. The door closes quickly behind me. A driver sits behind the wheel and pays me no attention. The gentleman beside me is a large white guy sitting with his legs crossed wearing a suit as well. With a dress hat and London Fog jacket to match, he takes a drag off his cigarette as he turns to look at me.

"Mr. Riggs?"

"Boy, everyone seems to know me, but I've never been introduced to any of you gangster wannabees."

"Mr. Riggs, I would suggest you be careful."

"And I would suggest you not tell me what to do. What do you want?"

The man is visibly agitated with my attitude, but I could care less. I don't appreciate being threatened. If they were going to kill me, they'd a done so before I ever entered this car.

"Mr. Riggs, we need the whereabouts of your father."

"Excuse me?"

"I said where is your father right now? And don't tell me he's dead because we know better."

An instantaneous shot of fear runs through my body. I try to act as if what he just said didn't faze me a bit. I hope I pulled it off but I can't be sure right now. As far as I knew, there were only three people that knew about this: Myself, Adam, and my father.

"I don't know who you are or what information you've been given, but my father is buried in a plot in Greencastle about an hour from here."

"Your father sir is alive and well. We know this and we need his location and we need it now."

"Sorry dude. I can't help ya. I buried the man personally two years ago. Buried him face up with a suit and tie neatly pressed. Even threw in a his old hunting cap and rifle."

"No Mr. Riggs; you buried John Merrick in that grave and we both know it. Your father has something we need. Again; we need his whereabouts."

The man looks past me and winks to his partner who has been standing just outside my door during our brief conversation. Suddenly the door opens and the cold steel of that handgun is pressed against the back of my head. It jerks my head forward. I stiff'n my neck in defiance and he pushes even harder. The man sitting beside me leans forward. His breath is horrendous and he could care less.

"Mr. Riggs. I will ask you one more time. Where is the location of your father?"

"I told you. He's dead. And if you think otherwise, killing me is not going to help you find him – is it?"

We stare at each other for what seems minutes. I know that one blink of his eye will signal his partner to pull the trigger and end my life here. I wait but he never gives that signal. He needs me but for what, I'm not sure.

Without warning, the pressure of the barrel disappears. The man leans back once again in his seat.

"Mr. Riggs. You have one week to give us the location of your dad."

"Are you not listening to me? My father is DEAD!"

The man ignores me totally.

"You have one week to give us his location.."

"Or what?"

"Well, since you don't seem to care about your own life, maybe you'd take an interest in this one."

The man reaches into his left coat pocket and hands me a photograph. The image on the picture is of a lady I haven't seen in awhile. The image is that of my mother.

"Where'd you get this?"

"I have a guy in Jacksonville just waiting on my signal."

"Signal for what?"

"You have one week Mr. Riggs. One week and that's all. We'll be in touch."

That is my queue to get lost and with pleasure. I exit the vehicle without delay. The gunman re-enters the car and speeds away without even saying goodbye. I stand there scared like a child – scared that this whole thing is getting out of hand. Who the hell are those guys? And how do they know that dad is alive? And what does my dad have that they would be interested in? Does he still have those diamonds? He told me he sold them. I can't go and see him now. They are obviously following me. And there's my mom down in Florida. What if I screw this up and she gets killed? If that happens; God help whoever crosses me then.

CHAPTER 22

I pedal my ass off back to the motel room and load up everything I brought with me into the Suzuki. I pay the front clerk and head back to my apartment. As I approach the complex, I look around and find no news media or fancy-dressed individuals hovering around.

I quickly enter my apartment and head straight for the bathroom. After going through a few drawers, I find the electric hair trimmer and begin the task of shaving my head, and getting rid of this God-awful orange hair that is attracting more attention than my mug on TV is.

Cutting one's hair off in their mid-40s can be somewhat nerve-racking. You just never know if it's going to grow back. It's almost like you're pushing your luck. I've always been thankful to God for the gift of a full head of the stuff. I know men who would give up their first born for what I have.

I finish the job in minutes and my Eurkea takes care of the mess. I stand back and admire my work. Not sure I like what I see but it's definitely an improvement over what was up there just a few moments ago.

I exit the bathroom and flop down on the couch in the living room. I start to look around and begin to notice things don't seem to be quite right.

I know I haven't been home for a day or two but since I'm the only one (other than the manager of this place) who holds a key to my apartment, no one should have been in here rooting around. But who's to say that guy in the black car and his annoying sidekick couldn't have gotten in here. Hell, they found me on my bicycle in the middle of nowhere.

What has caught my attention is my baseball trophy that was sitting on top of my entertainment center. It was still there but off to the side somewhat. That trophy represents a special time in my life. One of the few times I was victorious at something. I look at it often and know when it's been moved.

I was fourteen years old and playing ball in the town's pony league. The league consisted of four teams and I was on the Cardinals. We had a diverse group of guys from all walks of life and some could even play baseball. The coach was a local guy whose name escapes me now. I remember him having long brown hair and mustache. He kind of resembled a skinny version of Rollie Fingers. He wasn't the worst coach I ever had but I don't ever remember him actually teaching us anything. We kind of just went out and played the game.

It was 1976 and we started the year 0-3. To say we were bad did not do it justice. We were awful in every aspect of the game. So after our third loss, we held an impromptu meeting without the coach in the dugout. A few of us got up and voiced our displeasure over the embarrassing loses and vowed that it would stop – now. I'm not sure what supreme power took over, but for the rest of the season (thirteen games in all) we did not lose. I mean we were beating teams by multiple runs. After finishing 13-3 and winning the championship, I was handed a trophy that is probably not worth two dollars in materials. But that trophy has always symbolized to me that one can do just about anything they wish if they put their mind to it.

I refer to that trophy quite often and know its exact location all the time. I jump off the couch and walk over. I lift up the trophy and

examine it as I have done so many times in the past. It didn't take long
to find the listening device attached to the base of the statue.

I've seen these before. Used many in my police days to listen to the
bad guys in motel rooms and other places where bad guys are doing
bad things. But I'm not the bad guy here. I'm the good guy being
bugged by the bad guys. Life has an irony to it sometimes.

I immediately put the trophy back on the entertainment center
and make as little noise as possible. I know if there's one device in here,
there's probably one in each room to include my home phone. I finally
get the strength to come home and take charge of this mess and now
I feel like I did back at the motel room. I think it may be time for a
drive – a long drive.

———————

I hit the nearby interstate and head east. I opted for the highway
in lieu of the scenic back roads because one can pick a lane on the
highway and not be bothered by cars wanting to pass or negotiate the
number turns that wrap around the many farms in the area.

I ease back in the seat and start my analysis of this situation. I've never
been one to react well to situations. Shooting from the hip has never been
my forte. In order to excel in anything I attempt, I have always needed to
chew on things first. Usually twenty-four hours is enough time.

This is something I've learned about myself recently and would
have served me well in my early years. It's probably the main reason
why I've always finished second or third in everything I've ever done
competitively. In my teens, I shot archery as did every male member
of our family. I remember one time dad taking me to the state
championships in central Pennsylvania. After the second round of
competition, I found myself in second place. As in golf, they pair the
top three and they shoot the final round together.

The guy leading the tournament was a little odd, to say the least. I remember him having this bowl-style haircut and he walked like a girl. To make matters worse, he brought his girlfriend with him during the match. When I first saw this, I thought for sure she'd be a distraction and I could win this one hands down. I couldn't have been more wrong.

This guy was one of the most relaxed individuals I ever met. He'd put an arrow in the bulls-eye and then walk back to his girlfriend while I shot. During the wait, he and his lady friend would be kissing and rubbing each other's crouches behind me. It was apparent that the only person distracted from all of this was me. Arrow after arrow, target after target; this guy never missed and beat me like cornbread batter.

I left the tournament finishing third. My award was this little metal pin in the shape of a target. The thing was less than an inch in diameter. The winner got a trophy as tall as he was. I'll never forget it. After getting home, I took that pin and threw it deep in the cornfield in the back yard. I was humiliated and didn't want to be reminded of that day. The next week, I took along my girlfriend to the local archery range. All I heard the entire time was "when are we going to be done?" I shot the worst round of my life.

But no games being played now and not even my so-called girlfriend is helping me out. As I continue down the four-lane highway, it strikes me that I need to make a decision on what problem I want to concentrate my efforts on. The first is how I'm going to get a hold of dad and let me know that someone is on to our secret. I haven't seen them yet but I can feel them. They're following me right now and I sure as hell ain't going to the cabin until I am triple sure I'm not being tailed. The other problem of equal value is the fact that I'm a suspect in a triple murder that I had no involvement in.

Let's see; save my own hide or save my old mans'. Well; if I don't save my own hide, I sure as hell won't be able to save dads. So the decision is made. I need to speak with these FBI guys and cooperate with the investigation. Getting off their suspect list is priority number. I'll also need someone to watch out for my mom down in Florida.

CHAPTER 23

It's 2:30 in the afternoon and I'm pulling into a parking lot of a building in Bedford that I've passed a thousand times, but never took the time to identify. I earlier got in touch with the FBI and spoke with an Agent Barnhart who was heading up this so-called triple homicide. When I called, the agent was more than pleased to speak with me. In fact, she asked if I could make it down to the office today, and I agreed.

This building is old and has no identifying features at all. I admire the bureau for picking such a place. No one would ever know this was an FBI headquarters. This office has been here for over twenty years, and they have done a masterful job of keeping a low profile. I would assume the folks in the law enforcement community are aware of their presents, and since I've only been here a few months, I just haven't had the pleasure.

I enter the old-style Victorian building through a white metal door located in the back. I am immediately met by another metal door with a closed-circuit camera staring at me. I wave at the camera with a sarcastic smile letting them know I know they're watching and how much I don't care. I should be worried. I should be concerned that they could skip the questioning and just arrest me for these murders. They sure as hell have enough evidence. My only saving grace is that log and the GPS system that has me at a completely different location. I thought I would never say this but "Thank God" for computers and Bill Gates. My brother would be so proud.

Without doing or touching a thing, the lock on the door deactivates and I soon find myself looking at a woman in a very nice suit. The woman extends her arm and invites a handshake.

"Good Afternoon, Mr. Riggs. I'm Agent Barnhart with the FBI."

"Hello", as I return the handshake gesture. I normally don't shake hands with other people. I never quite understood the concept myself. I mean, think about it. You meet someone for the very first time and what do you do? You touch them. I don't know about you but I don't allow strangers in my space. I need a little time before that can happen.

But this lady seems nice and I am here to impress. Because if I don't, I'll be pounding out license plates the rest of my life.

"Follow me, Mr. Riggs."

"Yes, ma'am."

"I would appreciate it if you address me as Agent Barnhart."

"And why is that? You don't like ma'am?"

"No I don't. Mr. Riggs."

"I'll make a note of that."

The agent looks back over her left shoulder as she leads me down the corridor. Her demeanor is now one of confusion mixed with disgust as she never breaks stride. The woman is as tall as I am and appears to be quite fit underneath those nice threads. Her short haircut suggests she may walk on the other side of the fence. I'm okay with that. I've become somewhat tolerant of people over the years. However one chooses to live their lives is their business. I just didn't appreciate the attitude with the ma'am thing. In my world, that is a sign of respect: So much for making a good first impression.

We reach the end of the hall without a word being spoken between us. The only sound was that of the thick heels of her black leather dress shoes smacking the tile floor. The lack of additional conversation is definitely uncomfortable, but nothing I can't handle. I'll save the talking for later.

A right turn is quickly made and I find myself inside a small room equipped with a table and two chairs. It was your standard interrogation room. Concrete walls all around and not even a picture displayed to dress up the place. I know why they do this. Whenever questioning a suspect, they want that person focusing on the conversation at hand. Anything else in the room can be a distraction.

I take a seat without being asked. A tall young guy enters the room within seconds.

"Mr. Riggs. Thanks for coming down."

"No problem. We need to get this cleared up so I can get back to work and on with what little life I have."

After taking care of the handshaking ritual again, he sits down. The name tag on his suit jacket reads: Agent Outlaw.

"That's quite a name for a law enforcement officer." I say.

The man appears to be in his thirties and very tall. Not as tall as Hanson, but pretty close. His jet black hair and skin tone indicates he may be of Hispanic descent, but the voice has no accent at all.

"Yeah, we have a lot of fun with it around here."

Agent Outlaw takes a seat across from me. Like no other interview I've ever been involved in, this guy came in empty handed. No file, no pen in hand, no nothing. He doesn't even have a notebook with him. The female agent has taken up residency against the north wall and is apparently going to watch the show in lieu of getting involved.

"So, Mr. Riggs, just so you know; I have been following every aspect of this case since the first body was found. And I know about the pictures with you supposedly in a hunting suit standing over one of the guys. I know about all three bodies being found in your area. I know that the GPS system puts you nowhere near any of these deaths when they occurred. I also know that your fingerprints didn't show up on the phone where the reports of these deaths came in. And most importantly, I know you did not commit these crimes.

"Well good. I'm glad to hear it. I haven't heard that lately. Even my girlfriend is questioning my involvement in this crap."

"Sorry to hear that. So knowing all of these details leads me to one conclusion."

"And that is?"

"That you're being set up."

I nod in agreement.

"The next obvious question is who is going through with all of this to get you? Who is the individual responsible? But I'm not going to ask that question yet. Mr. Riggs, I want to know why."

The agent and I stare at one another.

"I have a feeling, Mr. Riggs, you know why this is happening. Why someone would go to these lengths to see you behind bars for the rest of your life. Someone out there really hates you, or you have something they want."

I hesitate and that is all he needs.

"Mr. Riggs, if you want to clear your name, I would suggest you start talking."

I vowed that I would never tell, but things are so bad that I may need to. It may be the only way to clear my name and also save my dad. I wonder if they would put him in jail for not coming forward when that guy in the shop was killed. It's too late now. I already hesitated. This agent is smart and knows I'm hiding something. No better time than now.

"Okay, but I want her gone from this room."

I point to Agent Barnhart who is still holding up the north wall.

"Why Mr. Riggs?"

"I'm not sure why. For some reason I don't trust her. And what I'm about to tell you is going to be confidential."

"Fair enough."

Agent Outlaw turns to his partner and nods his head. With a stare that could shoot bullets, she turns and soon leaves the room, making sure to slam the door shut harder than she has to.

Agent Outlaw then turns his attention back to me.

"So, Mr. Riggs – I'm listening."

"Okay, what I'm about to tell you goes no further than this room. Can you agree to that?"

"I can as long as no serious crimes have been committed."

"Well, I would say there may be a crime committed but nothing that I would categorize as serious."

"All right – go right ahead. I'm all ears."

"I am almost positive the reason I am being set up is because they want my father."

"Your father?"

"That's what I said – my dad."

"Mr. Riggs, I know about the incident two years ago up on the mountain. I was a new agent here but never really got involved in the case. I know from Hanson and my own follow-up they found your father shot to death in his shop back in Greencastle, and all that crap you went through in Wisconsin. So explain what you mean."

"I mean that my father is not dead."

Agent Outlaw was leaning forward when this interview started, but now is back in his seat looking at the wall behind me. His eyes affixed on something but what I don't know. There's nothing here. A few seconds go by and he looks at me once again, but with a serious glare.

"So if this is true, who was killed in the shop? And who the hell is six-feet under in a grave with your father's headstone sitting on top for display?"

"The night they came into my dad's shop, my dad was not home. But there was this guy who my dad had befriended, who would periodically come over to the shop and work on his cabinets. Dad was a part-time instructor at the nearby college and invited the guy over whenever he wanted. Wrong place at the wrong time – you know."

"So Riggs, you're telling me they executed the wrong man and the police didn't determine this?"

"That's what I'm saying. This guy was basically a homeless man living out of a motor home. He was the exact height, weight, and body size of that of my father. When they shot him, his entire head exploded and there was nothing left but a pile of goo. If you think I'm making all this up, go pull some prints and compar'em. I guarantee they'll match. But I'd appreciate it if you did this under the radar – so to speak."

"I'll need to get a set of prints from him."

"There's probably a thumb print out there or something you can find, maybe from a bank or when he gets his hunting license."

"Where is he, Mr. Riggs?"

"I don't know."

"You lie."

"That's right. I didn't agree to tell you everything, did I?"

"Do you know how much trouble you're in, if this is true? Why are you telling me this?"

"Because I just had two mobsters stop me out on Creek Road and gave me a week to disclose his whereabouts or they would start killing my family members one at a time – starting with my mom down in Florida. I need some help here, Agent. I was trying to handle this myself but I'm running out of options. I probably could deal with this if I just knew what the hell this is all about."

"Mr. Riggs, I know you're telling the truth. And the only way to save your dad is to take him into protective custody until we get to the bottom of this."

"He'll never go for it. He'll run like a scared rabbit from a fence line in October; I guarantee it. And why are you so quick to believe me. You're not playing me are you? I don't like to be played."

"No I'm not playing you. Your testimony today has possibly answered one of the burning questions I've had since I started this investigation."

"And what question is that?"

"What if I told you the name of the person who was buried in your father's grave."

"I'd say you were a mind reader because there are only three people who know his identity."

Agent Outlaw leans back once again in his seat and with his right hand, reaches for something in his right coat pocket. He soon returns to his upright position and holds his hand in front of me with the fingers closed and palm up. He's about to show me something that I could have never guessed in a million years.

As quickly as his hand appeared he slowly opened his fingers to display an item that I would have cared not to see ever again.

"It's a diamond Mr. Riggs."

I stare in disbelief. A diamond the size of a half dollar, a diamond that looked just like the one that Blue was after the day he tried to kill me. I didn't get a chance to look at them real closely that day, with me bleeding all over the ground and a 9mm pointed at my face.

"Where did you get that?"

"From the coat pocket of the first victim. Does it mean anything to you?"

"No."

"Bullshit it doesn't. This is why they tried to kill your dad isn't it? And why they were hell bent on hunting your ass down as well. They thought you had this."

"There was more than one."

"I wouldn't doubt it Mr. Riggs. We found this one with a note attached. You may think that that GPS system is keeping you from being arrested for these murders, but that note is the real reason."

"I've read the reports. There is no mention of this diamond being found."

"I know. I made sure they kept it out."

"So this is why everyone associated with me is off this case?

Agent nods his head.

"What did the note say?"

"I'm not at liberty to discuss that but I will keep my promise and take a stab at who's buried under your father's headstone."

"No one knows that."

"Would his name happen to be John Merrick?"

"What did the note say?"

"It read: 'In loving memory of John Merrick'."

A moment of silence was in order. I needed to search deep within myself and find the strength to trust the man who sits in front of me. It's a tough thing to do when so many are out to bury you and you have no idea who they are. This interview was a good idea. It's starting to become clear as to why this is happening. It all has to do with what took place two years ago. The mere mention of the name John Merrick in connection with these deaths is all I need to be convinced of that fact. My decision is made. I won't trust this man – this agent who is pretending to be my friend right now. It's not that he's not trustworthy, don't get me wrong, but he works for an agency that prides itself on integrity and following a strict code of ethics. I have no code of ethics – not anymore. Going forward, I will tell him just enough to keep his interest and with any luck, maybe I can use him to find the person responsible for setting me up to take this fall.

My thoughts are interrupted by the Agent who has grown uncomfortable with the silence.

"So, Mr. Riggs, are you going to tell me where your father is?"

"No I'm not. The problem is I'm not quite sure. He wants to keep it that way."

"You know I could lock you up right now for the information you've given me."

"You could but you won't."

"How can you be so sure?"

"Because you know that even if you locked me up, I wouldn't tell you anymore than I already have."

The agent leans forward in an aggressive manner.

"Mr. Riggs, I wouldn't try my patience if I were you."

I lean forward as well in defiance of his recent courage.

"Don't attempt to intimidate me. I've been fucked with by the best there is and you are not on that list. Now we can help each other solve this case. I need to get whoever's out to get him off my back. It's apparent that we are after the same person. Oh sure, you could charge me with these crimes but you know as well as I do you could never prove it. You help me, I'll help you. Deal?"

Agent Outlaw hesitates just as I thought he would. In order to help me out, he'll have to keep some things under his hat. This doesn't come easy for these FBI people – that code of ethics thing I mentioned earlier.

"Okay Mr. Riggs. I think we can work together. To start this relationship off right, let's say you start telling me about this John Merrick and how you came to know this man."

I spend the next ten minutes or so going over most of the details of my knowledge of this man. It's been two years but the details are still fresh in my mind. Outlaw still has no paper or pen to take notes. He is committing all this to memory. Either that or he has one of those digital recorders in his pocket. I know I would.

After telling my side of the story, It's now my turn to get some help.

"Okay Mr. Riggs, what information do you need?"

"No information for me. I need actual help."

"What kind of help?"

I tell the agent about the two men in the black Ford who threatened my mother. He listens in almost disbelief as I go over the details. I then show him the Polaroid photograph they surrendered in a poor attempt to scare me. The agent takes the photograph and examines it closely.

"What can I do for you on this?"

"Well, as far as the wannabee mobsters, I'm not too concerned about their threats now."

"Why?"

"Well, the photo you're holding is of my mother. But the house she is standing in front of is a place she owned several years ago. But just to be on the safe side, I'd like for you to have one of your agents down there just to keep an eye on her for me."

"Do you know where *she* lives?"

"Smartass!"

"Sorry – couldn't resist."

Just then, my cell phone rings. Well it's not actually a ring but a song from that new group Nickelback. Those dudes from Canada can really rock. I examine the number and recognize it to be my brother's cell number.

"Hey Adam, what's up?"

"What's up with you? I hear you're about to do some jail time for killing a bunch of people."

"It'll never happen. I'm too fast for 'em. And besides, I didn't do it."

I get no response and a few seconds of static transmits through my earpiece.

"Are you in town Adam?"

"Yeah I am. When's the last time you checked on dad."

"About two weeks ago. I haven't stopped by lately because of all this mess I've been dealing with. Why?"

"Cause I'm at the cabin right now. You need to get over here right away."

"Why – what's going on?"

"Just get over here – quick."

CHAPTER 24

I left the FBI building quickly and calmly. The agent was listening in on my conversation but had no idea who I was talking to. He did ask and I told him it was my dentist reminding me of my appointment for later in the week. He didn't buy that for a second and I didn't expect him to. It was my way of saying; mind your own business.

After being let out of the building (and they have to let you out with all the security in this place), I head around to the back side of the mountain. It is the long way to dad's cabin. I have to take this way. It wouldn't surprise me a bit that the agent would have someone tail me for the rest of my life. I liked the guy but I don't trust him. Then again, I don't trust most people.

I've been on the road for just under an hour, stopping periodically to make sure no one is following. The only car I saw the entire ride back here is Elmer's old Ford LTD station wagon. You remember Elmer; the guy who I told to shoot the PETA woman if she started following him again. I recall my encounter with her the other day in the morgue. I don't even want to know what happen to her. I can't imagine Elmer would have killed her. He is so old and shaking, he can barely hold up that bow besides putting an arrow into a moving target.

I finally reach the cabin and make my familiar turn off of Barker Road. I ease back the long driveway thinking about my brother and what he wanted to talk to me about – and quick. Was there something wrong? DID THEY FIND MY DAD? This thought immediately caused my right foot to lunge forward, which just happened to be lying on the gas pedal at the time.

As I make the right onto dad's long driveway, it occurs to me how long I've been off work. Next week starts the gun deer season here in Pennsylvania. I've been suspended for almost a month now from the game commission and still a free man. I can only surmise that the FBI team can't put a case together against me. I could have told them that.

I round the first bend and ponder my brother's phone call. He wouldn't tell me what the problem was or even if there was a problem at all. His voice sounded cold and controlled: not at all like him.

In a few minutes, I place my car in park. A quick look at the cabin finds Adam standing at the doorway. I can only imagine the old man inside yelling at him about letting all the heat out. Heat is a premium up here and doesn't come cheap.

I make my way up the walkway.

"What's up Adam? You sounded strange on the phone."

"Come see for yourself."

I follow Adam inside.

"Where's the Asian lady?"

"What lady?"

"Dad had some lady living with him. I wasn't too crazy about it when he was supposed to be up here undercover."

"Well if there was someone else living here, they're long gone by now."

"Adam, what's going on? Where's the old man?"

"Back patio."

I make my way through the small living room and see the back of my dad's head resting against his favorite chair.

"Hey dad – how's it going?"

"As I round the right side of his chair, I get no response from my question."

"Dad, wake up?"

I look and see his chin buried in his chest. There's saliva dripping from his mouth and nose along with a familiar smell that I would care not to inhale ever again. I immediately fall to my knees. It appears he died about two days ago.

"Oh no."

"I found him just like that Marvin. I can't see any signs that he was killed. It looks to me like he might have had a heart attack or something."

"And you know we'll never know Adam. He's already dead as far as the world's concerned."

"So what do we do now?"

"I'm not sure. I need a moment."

I zip up my jacket and step outside to collect my thoughts. Neither Adam nor I have any tears left to shed. We used them all up the last time he died.

I now stand on the uncovered front porch of what I used to call my dad's place. It was not something I could say out loud but a comforting thought whenever I needed strength. Just knowing he was nearby always gave me the courage to move forward. But now he's gone, and this time there's no doubt about it.

I start to plan what Adam and I need to do here. I can't help but wonder where the lady friend went to and if she had anything to do with my father's second death. But since we can't call the authorities and initiate an investigation for obvious reasons, we'll need to place him in the ground and get on with our lives.

I finish my cigarette and re-enter the cabin where I find Adam sitting in the living room.

"So what do we do, Marvin?"

"We'll need to bury him in the back somewhere, which isn't going to be easy."

"Why's that? We'll just dig a hole."

"It's winter Adam. The ground is frozen up here?"

"Oh yeah. It would take a backhoe to get a hole deep enough."

"I know. We could put him in the freezer until spring and then bury him."

"And what if someone just happens upon this place and finds him in there? I'm in enough trouble already. One more body found in my general vicinity and they'll throw away the key, especially if they find him. You and I will be answering questions until we're old and gray."

"We're already old and gray."

"Well, really old and gray then."

A few minutes of silence looms inside the cabin. We are both trying hard to come up with a solution to this problem. We need to put dad somewhere so the authorities won't find him. I begin to kick myself for telling that FBI guy that dad was alive. If I'd only held off one more day before telling him that, I'd have one less issue to deal with. But how was I to know? I'm not psychic. My father is dead and for sure this time. I take comfort in knowing we together were able to give him a few more years on this earth.

"Hey Adam, let's do this. Let's put him in the freezer and push it up against the wall here in the kitchen. We'll put a padlock on it and cover the thing with a table cloth. Since I need to stay out of the public eye as it is and no one knows about this place, I'll just stay up here. When the spring comes and the ground thaws, we can bury him then. What do ya think?"

"Hey, if you can sleep at night with a dead man in the house, by all means go for it."

"It's not just a dead man – its dad."

"Still, it's a good plan."

————————

Moving a dead body is much more than just picking it up and placing it where you want to. The human body works much like the engine in your car. When the car is running, you have the oil pump moving that special lubricant throughout every nook and cranny, keeping all the parts cool and free of friction. When the engine is stopped, all the oil settles to the bottom of the pan and patiently waits for the next turn of the key. The human body works much in the same way. When the engine is running, the heart is your oil pump moving that vital liquid throughout the body, keeping your parts fed and in good working order. The one big difference between the two is that once the body shuts off, there's no ignition switch to restart it. Within minutes, you are considered dead and nothing but the hand of God himself is going to bring you back.

It'd be nice if the body was equipped with an oil pan to help catch some of those decaying body fluids. No such luck. My dad has been sitting in this chair for a minimum of two days. I tried to warn Adam before he yanked on dad's arm and hoisted him over his shoulder.

"Holy shit! What is that smell?"

"You are correct. And since it's already running down your back, you might as well just keep walking toward the freezer."

Adam continues to walk across the kitchen as I hold the lid to the freezer open. Never heard a man gag so much and not throw up. He reaches the freezer and with respect, labors as he lays dad face up onto a blanket of deer steaks and tenderloins.

"This doesn't seem right, Marvin."

"I know, but we'll do the proper thing this spring. This is just temporary."

I quickly close the lid to the freezer.

"Hey Adam, there *is* a place on this thing for a padlock."

"If you need me to Marin, I can run into town later and pick one up."

"No need to Adam. I've got one at the apartment we can use. I'll pick it up when I go there this afternoon. Need to get some stuff anyways."

"Are you going to move in here for the time being?"

"Might as well. I need to stay low and out of sight. And living here, where absolutely no one knows about this place, is just as good as any."

"You *hope* no one knows about this place."

"Why do you say that?

"We still don't know what killed dad."

"It appears natural Adam. I wouldn't be too concerned."

"Okay. You're the one that's going to be sleeping here with a body in the freezer."

"I'll be fine. Don't worry. I've got my cell if things go to hell."

I break out my new phone, which catches my brother's attention. He quickly grabs it and starts to examine the features.

"Marvin, why don't you have the locator set on this thing?"

"I don't know. Maybe I don't want to be located. By the way, what are you doing up here anyway? Rifle season doesn't start for another week."

"I thought I'd come up and do some scouting, and check on the old man while I was at it. I still might do that. Not much I can do around here right now."

"That's true. Are you coming back?"

"Nah, I'll head back to the house after I'm done."

"Okay."

Adam zips up his jacket and heads for the front door. Before he exits, I get his attention.

"Hey Adam, do you know what the old man did with those two diamonds we almost got killed over?"

"Dad told me he sold them to some shady character in town."

"That's what he told me too. What if I told you I just saw one of them?"

"Bullshit."

"I did. And guess who has possession of it?

"Who?"

"An FBI agent. And what if I told you the diamond they have was found in the shirt pocket of the first victim up on the mountain?"

Adam stares and says nothing.

"And, oh yeah, it gets better. There was a note attached to the diamond that made reference to John Merrick."

Adam pauses before he speaks.

"You're not making any of this up, are you?"

"Nope."

"I don't want to know anymore Marvin. You need to keep your head down, your eyes open, and that gun loaded. And hears your cell phone."

Adam tosses it to me from a few feet away, which I confidently catch.

"I'll see ya in few weeks."

Adam quickly exits the cabin and before I can reach the window, he is down the driveway heading for Martin's Hill. I can't really blame him for running. If I could – I would.

CHAPTER 25

Adam's been gone for about an hour now and I don't expect him back. Putting dad in the freezer really freaked him out. So much so he didn't even attempt to get the body fluids off his jacket. I doubt any deer in their right mind will get within a mile of him with that smell swirling around.

I spend the next hour or so digging around the cabin looking for something to cover the freezer. I finally find a table cloth in the hallway closet and a vase in the living room. I'm no interior decorator but I was able to disguise our make-shift morgue into something that resembles a kitchen table. Out-of-sight, out-of-mind.

The sun has just made its final appearance for the day. It would be a good time to head over to the apartment and pick up a few things, including a padlock for this freezer.

I start out with my headlights off. I'm getting somewhat paranoid with being seen. If I'm going to stay here, I'll need to take extra precautions to stay invisible. No one can know about this place. I still don't understand why dad would take the risk of having that girlfriend back here. I can't help but wonder where she went. If she's still living in town, I'm sure I'll eventually run into her. There are not many Asian folks living around here.

I reach the hard road and make my left turn in route to the apartment. Just as I flick on the headlights, my cell phone goes off. I quickly secure the device from the breast pocket of my winter jacket and recognize the number right away.

"Hi Mandi"

"MARVIN, THANK GOD YOU'RE STILL ALIVE."

"Yeah – did you hear differently?"

"YES. Marvin your apartment – its - its gone. They found a…"

My cell goes off again and mutes whatever Mandi is trying to tell me. The new call is from Hanson.

"Mandi, hang on just on second - okay?"

Without waiting for a reply, I switch the call over.

"Hello"

"MARVIN, YOU'RE STILL WITH US. HOLY SHIT."

"Well yeah. Mandi's on the other line surprised as well that I'm still upright. What's going on?"

"You don't know?"

"Know what?"

"Marvin, someone just blew up your apartment."

"WHAT?"

"You need to get over there as soon as possible. They have a body there and everything."

"I'm on my way."

I click the phone back to Mandi.

"Mandi? Mandi!"

The line is dead.

———

Twenty minutes later I arrive at the city limits, which is usually a good thirty-minute trip. It's funny how being notified that your apartment just blew up and everyone thinks you're dead will increase the weight on your right foot while driving. I scan the skyline and see smoke billowing from the direction of what I used to call home. Within a minute or two, I make the left into my apartment complex and find fire trucks everywhere, along with a number of uniformed officers.

I quickly park my car and take a closer look at the damage. Black smoke continues to rise from the ashes of everything I once owned. My entire place is gone. There is also some damage to the adjacent apartments as well. My thoughts are many. What happened? Who did this? Did any of my neighbors get hurt? My questions will soon be answered as I see Agent Outlaw approach with a surprised look on his face. I exit my vehicle.

"Marvin! Well that answers one of my questions."

"What question is that?"

"If that was you lying dead in the living room."

"There's someone in there?"

"Yeap. Do you have any idea who it might be? Maybe your father?"

"I don't have any idea and it's definitely not dad. I guarantee you that. What the hell happen?"

"We're not sure yet. It could be as simple as a gas leak."

"I doubt it. Nothing in my world is that simple."

"So why were you not here?"

"I was out scouting deer with my brother."

"But you told me during our interview that you don't hunt anymore."

"That's right I don't, but I do enjoy the woods and spending time with my brother."

Have you ever tried to explain something to someone and no matter how hard you try, they're not buying it? Agent Outlaw was nodding his head in agreement but his eyes were telling a different story. He's no longer going to be a problem. He's going to spend most of his time attempting to find my father. Now that he's truly dead; happy hunting.

"So where ya going stay now?"

"I - I don't know. I guess I'm going to have to call a friend."

"Do you have any?"

"I guess I'll find out. Will you let me know who's lying inside my apartment?"

"Sure will, once we make the identification."

"Good. I'll make it a point to keep my cell on."

I enter my vehicle and start her up to get some heat going. I grab a cigarette from a nearby pack in the center console and start packing it in. The packing ritual helps with the stress level. The feeling of being pursued is upon me once again, just like it was two years ago. Somebody wants me dead – again. And just like before, I'm not quite sure why. Then there's this diamond issue, which I can't help anyone with because the police have it.

I start to remember what took place when they wanted the huge buck my dad shot. It was my aggressiveness that saved my life that time. I didn't just lie down and let them finish me off. I fought them and I won. I need to find that strength again; that motivation to take out whoever gets in my way. It's the only thing these people relate to.

I catch movement to my left and watch as Hanson approaches my car. I roll down the window halfway.

"Marvin – any answers for us?"

"Not a one."

"Somebody wants you dead."

"As usual. Seems to be the status quo for me lately."

"Do you have any idea who's inside your place?"

"None. I need a favor Mark."

"What's that?"

"Do you have an extra gun on ya?"

"Yeah – Why?"

"I need it."

"For what?"

"What do you think? Look at my place."

"Marvin, there have been more dead bodies found since you arrived in this town, than in the prior one hundred year history of its existence. I am not giving you a gun so you can increase that number."

"As a favor Mark, someone is trying to erase me and they don't care who they hurt. I need a weapon. I promise that I won't purposely shoot anyone unless they shoot at me first."

Hanson looks at me and slowly stares at the ashes of my apartment. With a long, deep breath, he turns and walks to his patrol vehicle. He reaches inside and retrieves a piece from underneath the driver's seat and returns to my vehicle.

"Okay here. But I'm not the one who gave it to ya. Deal?"

"Deal – Hey, this is my service weapon."

"I know. If you get caught with it, you didn't get it from me."

"Thanks Mark. I owe you."

"That's an understatement."

I secure my new piece of hardware in my crotch and quickly exit the parking lot with Mandi on my mind. She didn't answer when I called back. I dial her number once more and with one ring, she answers.

"Hey, where'd you go? I tried calling you back."

"I guess you were in a bad spot Marvin."

"Hey, I'm homeless."

"And?"

"And I need a place to stay."

"So whose the person burnt up in your apartment?" she inquired with a cold tone of voice.

"I don't know. Boy, you were so concerned about me ten minutes ago and now."

"Are you sure you don't know who's in there?

"Honest to God Mandi I have no idea."

"Are you sure?"

"What do you mean am I sure? Of course I am. What the hell are you getting at?"

"Sure you ain't seeing someone else?"

"Goodbye Mandi. I appreciate all your help – Not."

CHAPTER 26

It's late Thursday morning when I arrive at a place that should be familiar to me, but I chose a different path in life. Wilson College, just outside of Thiensville, is your typical community institution with smaller classes to go along with the small tuition fees. If I would have chosen to attend college after high school, this is where I would have gone – but I didn't, and I have paid for that decision ever since. Struggling to make ends meet has been a twenty-five year ordeal that continues to this day. Who would have thought that hard work was no longer an option?

I was cursed growing up in my household watching my father. He was a man who (from what I have heard) barely finished high school. My mom told me a story once where my dad was given two job offers and was having a difficult time deciding which one to take. They were a newly married couple and I was weeks away from being much more than an idea. My father was faced with the decision to take a job as a custodian or accept an apprenticeship program at Mack Trucks. Now you would think that this was a no-brainer but not so. They needed money and the custodian job was paying more than the one at Mack.

Now according to my mom, dad was leaning toward the custodian position but my mom insisted that the apprenticeship would pay greater dividends down the road. My father reportedly took the Mack job under some protest.

Since that day, I watched a man with a high school diploma work his way up at a company where he eventually became a senior VP in the engineering department. Never a day a college did he waste. I witnessed this as a young man and saw that we were better off than most financially. I came to the conclusion that no college degree was required to excel in this world. And with that attitude, I barely squeaked by high school myself. I don't know the exact number but I do know that I finished fifteenth or twentieth from the bottom of my class of one hundred and sixty-five students. At the time, I didn't care.

Now this philosophy would have served me well if the world would have stayed the way it was. But no such luck. Bill Gates came along and changed everything. And somewhere along the way, we decided to let every one waltz into this country, causing our population to explode. I believe those two combinations changed this world forever. With computers taking over ever aspect of our lives and more and more people chasing the so-called "American Dream" companies found themselves with hundreds of choices in who they hire.

And then came the requirements or conditions for employment. All of the sudden you needed a college degree to do anything. One to ride on the side of a garbage truck and empty garbage cans; one in custodial engineering so one could effectively mop a damp floor; and I once saw an ad for a trucking firm looking for a dispatcher to work the midnight shift – bachelor's degree requirement. They would start you at $8.50 per hour. Someone wake me up when this is over.

During this transition, I was so busy working and raising kids, I failed to see what was happening. Like Rip Van Winkle in the fairy tale, one day I woke up and I was obsolete. I was a dinosaur in a modern world with no one taking me seriously. My experience in life had no bearing on employers who sat in big offices judging applicant after applicant on credits instead of character. I could go back to school but at my age, what's the point. I have taken a few college courses along the way and always find myself irritated with instructors who don't know if their ass is punched, bored, drilled, or reamed. And most of the students in their twenties who just think they are so much better than everyone else because they've planted their ass in a seat for years. Give me a hard-working Joe with work experience and a great attitude any day of the week.

Well so much for my blowing off steam. I need to get back to work here. I'm being pursued by person(s) unknown. Or maybe I do know them and it just hasn't been revealed to me yet. Either way, I've got work to do today.

I exit my Suzuki and check myself out in the reflection of my driver's side window. This three-piece suit is looking sharp on me today. I picked it up at the warehouse store in Cumberland this morning, especially for the occasion. And since every piece of clothing I own is now nothing more than dust, I will need to break open a piggy bank or two and get some replacements. Stupid-ass me didn't purchase any renters insurance when I got that place.

I weave my way through the parked cars and check to make sure I have my badge and paperwork. I'm about to include acting as another one of my talents. My goal here is to gain some access to a file that is buried somewhere in this building.

I remember my father telling me the day we came back from a hunting trip and John Merrick was inside his shop. He told Adam and me that he was volunteering his time at the college to teach woodworking. John was one of his students. Anyone who attends a college must complete an application of some kind. I need to get a copy of that application and see what I can learn about this mysterious individual who has been the cause of my ills here lately. But I'm smart enough to know that with the privacy act laws in place throughout this country, they won't let anyone just walk in here and take a peek at it. I'll need to be someone of importance – hence the acting.

I enter the admissions office and meet a middle-aged woman sitting behind a waist-high counter. She greets me with a smile that interrupts my presentation, and I'm not sure why. I've seen this person before but her face does not register a name right away.

"May I help you sir?"

"Yes. I – I want to review a file that you have here at the college."

"Marvin – Marvin Riggs? Is that you?"

The woman knows my name and my first thought is she watches the news as well.

"I'm sorry ma'am – I don't know who you are."

"It's me, Roxanne Lancer from high school. Do you remember me?"

The name instantly takes me back almost thirty years; back to a time when running from the cops and violating your girlfriend in the backseat of your car was nothing more than a game. I had just turned sixteen years old when Roxanne and I were out on a weekend drive through the backwoods of my hometown. There was a special spot off of Turkey Road that one could back their car into and be invisible from all traffic. Roxanne and I visited this spot a few times during a brief relationship. She was my first and she knew it.

"Wow, Roxanne. It's been a long time."

"It sure has Marvin. Where the hell have you been?"

"Just about everywhere; How about you?"

"I never left town. I married a guy who owns a construction company, had three kids, and we're about to retire and do some traveling. How about you?"

"Divorced, two daughters, and just living life."

"That doesn't sound very exciting Marvin."

"You should have been with me the last couple of years. Never a dull moment. So you went to college?"

"Yeap, got a Ph.D in physics."

"And you work here?"

"I don't need to work. My husband takes care of that."

Now why in the world would someone spend eight plus years in school to obtain the highest degree you can achieve and not use it. How stupid is that?

"What's your degree in Marvin?"

"What makes you think I have one?"

"Well you have to have one."

"No you don't. You just have to know what you're doing."

"And what do you do?"

"I'm an investigator with the Pennsylvania Game Commission."

I take the opportunity to flash an extra badge I have. Gates took mine at that bullshit interrogation a few weeks ago but I had an extra silver one when I worked back at the police department in Florida. I was supposed to turn it in.

"I'm actually here on official business."

"Really?"

She appears to still be recovering from my announcement that I have survived this many years without attending college. She's definitely not the same Roxanne I knew in the backseat of my car. Time and money has kept her appearance up but there's nothing attractive about her anymore.

"We are investigating a missing person's case, and we received information that this person attended this college."

"Who's the student?"

"John Merrick."

"John, I remember him. He's the one who had a learning disability. He came here to study one of the labor positions. I think it was woodworking."

"I'm not sure what he studied, but I need to briefly look at this file to see if we can come up with a clue to find this guy."

"Sure Marvin. Give me one second."

Roxanne struts over to the other side of the office. I thought for sure she was going to speak with someone first, and then I would have to pull out this makeshift court order and convince these college punks that this was legit. Roxanne surprises me as she struts back to the counter with the file in hand. How lucky am I?

"Here ya go. There's not much in here."

"I see that. Just an application and that's it. Can you make a copy of this for me and I'll just take it with me?"

"Sure."

Roxanne struts her way over to the copier. If I didn't know better, I'd say she was trying to get my attention. I'm in my late forties now. She'll have to do better than this.

"Here ya go. Is there anything else you need?"

"No. I appreciate your help. It was nice seeing you again."

"You too."

I depart quickly and feel as if I just left an environment where I didn't quite fit in. I think more folks would be open to college if the atmosphere were that of acceptance of all persons who want a degree. They say they do, but they don't. To get into a so-called "good" college one must drop down at least ten grand or more a year to attend. That eliminates about sixty percent of the folks out there. So be it – I'll just work for a living. I'm not crazy about these three-piece suits anyways.

I exit the parking lot and head toward my hometown. I figure while I'm in the area, I might as well take a ride through some familiar territory. I'd like to find a nice, quiet place to review this application – and I know just the place.

CHAPTER 27

The road back to my special place is narrow; more so than I remember as a kid. Of course everything seems smaller these days for some reason. One has to be careful with oncoming traffic because there is barely enough asphalt for two cars.

After a few miles, I reach the long driveway back to my refuge – the sportsman's club here in Greencastle. It's a place I assumed as a kid had been here for centuries. The website advises otherwise -established in 1945. It's where my dad introduced me to the game of archery. It's the main recreation here, but not the only thing one can do. The archery range is on your left as you enter and the skeet range to the right. The festival grounds are straight ahead where each year they hold the "Ox Roast." This annual event is where you can play games and eat ox roast sandwiches till you puke. They were fifty cents each back then, and for that awesome price you got a serving of succulent beef on a hamburger bun. My mouth starts to water just thinking about having a plate in front of me.

If fishing is your forte, just drive down to the bottom of the hill to the huge pond on the right. Many a weekend our family would set up on the banks with lawn chairs and coolers and bring in more bluegills than we could eat. It wasn't hard either. All you needed was a worm, hook, and a bobber and you were in business.

Just before hunting season, if you needed to sight-in your hunting rifle, one can stop off at the shooting range to your left for some target practice.

But today I'm going to shoot a round of archery. One of things the fire didn't take from me was my bow. For whatever reason, I have always stored that in the trunk of my car. Never know when the urge to fling a few arrows into the air or at a target will come along.

I pull into the parking lot adjacent to the clubhouse and observe only a few cars here today. The weather is kind of cool this morning and being a weekday, most folks are working. I should be working too. I should be out patrolling Martin's Hill. I left everything back in Wisconsin to do just that. But instead I'm here trying to figure out who's got it in for me. If I don't solve this quickly, I may never see this place again.

I turn off the ignition and lean back in the seat. I retrieve the copy of John's application from my jacket pocket in hopes of coming up with some information that will put this fiasco to rest. The copy is barely readable but I manage. John listed his home with the address from the college. That would make sense since one is living in a motor home. Wherever you're at, at any one particular time is home I guess.

I continue down the form line by line and his physical description is amazingly similar to my dad. 5' 10" in height, 180 pounds, brown hair, blue eyes. It's no wonder the detectives working that day didn't investigate the body closer. Based on this information, they probably assumed this was an open and shut case as to the identity of the body.

I reach the last section of the document and find what I'm looking for. The college had asked John to list references. He listed one name - a name I've seen before. The name of a person I've been suspicious of since the night I found a folder with John's name on it: Dr. Joseph

Winger. And in the next box over where it asks to list the relationship of the reference: Uncle.

I immediately grab my phone and hit the speed dial for Hanson. I get a voice mail and decide not to leave a message. This is huge clue. What are the odds of running into a man who is related to the one person who took two bullets for my dad? I need to learn more about Dr. Winger. Is he involved in this somehow? Is he the one responsible for the vial of blood that's missing? I suspect he is. The next time we meet, it won't be in the dead of night. I'll be marching my ass into his office in the morning and get some answers.

I exit the vehicle and grab my bow from the trunk. I look around and everything's the same. The practice targets are right where I left them thirty years ago. The path back to target number one still borders the driveway. As I start down the path, the memories of this place flood my brain. This place was the main reason I stayed out of trouble in my youth. It gave me a sense of accomplishment and brought the three men in our small family closer.

At one time, my dad was the president of the archery association here. That was a good time for me. Everyone looked up to my dad in that position and I was treated with respect; not because I deserved it but because I was the son of the president. I got a taste of what it must be like to be the son of Ronald Reagan or the daughter of George W. Bush.

I arrive at target number one and again it's right where I left it. I place an arrow on the rest and adjust my sights for thirty-five yards. I pull back on the bow string and hear the pulley's on my compound creek from not being used for so many years. I steady my aim and soon release the arrow just as the sight pin reaches the bull's-eye. With great anticipation I watch my arrow soar through the cool November air on its way to my desired destination. The arrow then clips the top edge of a sheet of plywood that is used to keep the rain off the target. My projectile is redirected upward to the sky, never to be seen again. I missed the entire target by two feet. I can hear the voice of my father in my head as I stand there in disbelief. "That one was a bit high Marky." Marky was a nickname I inherited from an old friend who we called "Doc." He wasn't a doctor or anything close to it. I think he worked for the railroad. I chuckle at the memory and enjoy my time with it.

Your standard archery tournament round consists of twenty-eight targets in all. Here at the club they have them divided into the 1st fourteen and the 2nd fourteen, better known as the 1st half and the 2nd half. I'm shooting the front half this morning.

You're allowed four arrows per target and the goal (obviously) is to place each arrow in the bull's-eye. Each arrow that finds its way to that mark earns the shooter five points, making a possible score of twenty points per target. A perfect half round of archery will reward the archer with a score of 280. I'm on target number ten and my scorecard has me barely breaking the one hundred mark. I am disgusted with my round but not surprised. I haven't shot in many years and this game is definitely not one where you just pick up where you left off.

I take a seat on a nearby bench to catch my breath before attempting this target. There's nothing flat about this country. During my breather, I can't help but notice how much archery and the game of golf have in common. Both sports have a set number of rounds; both require their select projectiles to land at a prescribed destination. Both require many acres of land to set up the course, and both have a tendency for the participants to launch their equipment in frustration. Archery is a very tedious game that mandates the shooter to be consistent with every shot, but flexible enough to allow for changing weather conditions and the slope of the terrain. For those who are inconsistent (like me), arrows typically go where you don't want them to.

After about five minutes of rest, I return to the line and place an arrow on the bow rest. This target is a 65-yarder that slopes downward into a small gulley. I know from experience that I'll need to hold the sight pin underneath the bull's-eye because sixty-five yards downhill is more like sixty-three. I raise the bow and pull back on the string. I hold for a second trying to get a true bead on my target, when the snap of a tree branch echoes behind me. I also know from experience that branches don't snap by themselves. It requires pressure from an outside source to make such a sound. I haven't seen anyone on the course this morning and suddenly become concerned with my surroundings.

I continue to hold the bow at full draw, looking to my left and to my right in hopes of determining the source of the noise. After several glances in both directions, I look upward and into a small mirror that I have mounted on the upper limb of my compound bow. The source of the pressure that broke the branch has now been identified.

At full draw I wheel around and hone my sights on a gentleman I've met before.

"May I help you with something?"

Standing about twenty yards away is the man who held a gun to my head and forced me into a car along side the road about a week ago. The partner of the man who said he would hurt my mother if I didn't reveal the location of my dad. The man appears to be wearing the same black suit as before, along with the same handgun down by his side.

"Did I surprise you?"

"Yes Mr. Riggs, you did. I'm impressed."

"What do ya want?"

"Nothing, we're just watching you."

"It appears you're by yourself today. Like I said before, you guys are wasting your time and mine – he's dead."

"We'll see."

"I should stick you right here and now."

"You could try but I'd have a bullet in you before the arrow would get here. Besides; I've spent the last hour watching you shoot. You really suck."

Now he's pissed me off. He wouldn't have made such a comment in my hay-day. But I can no longer trade verbal shots with this guy. My arm is tiring quickly and if I don't let off this bowstring soon, I'm gonna lose my grip.

Without saying a word, the man turns and walks back the way he came. I release my hold and wonder why he wanted me to see him? Is he trying to scare me? Who is he working for? This guy is a follower for sure. He's doing what he's told to do.

I decide my trip down memory lane is over. I need to get the hell out of here. I skip the next five targets and run back to my vehicle. Upon my arrival, I expect to see all my tires flat, but they're not. I quickly load my gear into the trunk and head straight for driver's side – and stop. I discover my driver's side door is ajar and the vehicle unlocked. I take a quick scan of my immediate surroundings and nothing has changed from an hour ago. The same cars are still parked here, the same deserted practice range. The only thing that is different is my door is open.

Being a former cop, I am religious about making sure my stuff is locked up. It is so engraved in my subconscious that I do it as effortlessly as one will blink an eye or wipe sweat from their brow. In my police days, I've taken so many theft reports that I am convinced that if it's not nailed down, they'll find a way to take it.

My thoughts now race back to visions of my apartment that lie in ashes back in Bedford. Has someone been messing with my car? If I open this door, will I be blown to bits? I begin to examine the edges of the door and find nothing unusual. I then get down on my hands and knees, checking the bottom door frame and the undercarriage. I can find nothing out of the ordinary. Everything looks as it did when I left, except for this door that has mysteriously not been closed all the way. That little voice inside my head tells me to back away. It's screaming at me that something is wrong. I have learned from my forty plus years on this planet that the voice is never wrong. Everyone has it. It just takes time for one to understand what it's trying to say.

I walk around to the other side of the clubhouse for the purpose of using my cell phone. I guess I watch too much television and have seen movies where bombs have been detonated by the use of a cell. I'm not taking any chances. That voice continues to scream in my ear. I hit the speed dial and wait from an answer.

"Hello."

"Hanson, its Marvin."

"Marvin. Where are you?"

"Greencastle."

"Where's that?"

"It's in Pennsylvania dummy."

"I never heard of it. Why are you there?"

"Because it's my hometown. I told you this before."

"I don't remember. So what's up?"

"I need some help again."

"So what else is new?"

"Mark, I'm serious. I know you're not going to believe this but I think someone's been tinkering with my car."

"What do you mean tinkering?"

"I mean tinkering. I think someone may have planted a bomb or some explosive device on it. I just got back from shooting a round of archery and found my driver's door ajar. I always lock my stuff up Mark – you know that."

"Yes you do. And just so you know, they determined it was no gas leak that blew up your place. C4 was the culprit and lots of it."

"No shit? Did you determine yet who was inside?"

"Not yet. They're still working on it. What do ya need out there Marvin?"

"I need to know if they have a bomb squad that works this area to come up and look at this."

"I'll have to check. I could send my mother-in-law over and have her open the door for ya."

"You are Mr. Funnyman today. I bet you'd change your tune if your wife heard that."

"Keep you cell on Marvin – I'll make some calls."

"Okay, but try to hurry. I left out one thing in my story."

"What's that?"

"Remember those pretend gangsters that cornered me about a week ago? One of them snuck up on me in the woods."

"No shit. What happen?"

"Not a whole lot. He made sure I saw him thou and then just walked away."

"Stay put. I'll call you right back."

CHAPTER 28

Two hours go by before a plain looking Ford pulls into the parking lot. Before I can walk over and greet the two gentlemen who are wearing camouflage khakis and flack jackets, Hanson in his state-owned vehicle pulls in behind them. He exits the vehicle and immediately starts walking my way. I see he brought along a friend with him – Agent Outlaw. The two approach with the looks of concern on their faces.

"You okay Marvin?" Hanson asks.

"Not really. Someone's messing with my car and I ran out of cigarettes an hour ago."

"Can't help you with the cigarette dilemma but those two guys at your vehicle are from the Franklin County bomb squad. They are the best in the business. Are you sure something's up?"

"I'm positive. I would never suspect a bomb, but since I'm homeless because of one, I'm a little on edge."

"Are you sure the guy in the woods is the same one with the gun back in Bedford?" Outlaw interjects.

"No doubt about it. He was even holding the same gun down by his side. He was only twenty some yards from me. What really bothers me is he wanted me to see him. He wanted me to run back to my car."

"Did he say anything about your dad?"

Hanson swings his head toward Outlaw and then toward me just as quick.

"What about your dad?" Hanson asks.

An uncomfortable few seconds goes by as I try to come up with a lie to get myself out of having to explain this. The last time I felt this way was when my ex-wife found out about my personal extra curricular activities. Needless to say, it wasn't one of my better days. Our secret is starting to unravel. The truth is rearing its ugly head for everyone to see. The bible says that the truth will set you free. This truth won't. This one will lock me up or at minimum, cause me to report to a probation officer every week for the next few years. I wish Adam was here to take some of the brunt of this. But what's the use in both of us going to jail. I'll need him to bail me out. And besides, it's not like I killed anyone.

Just as I start to form my first word and reveal the secret of my father to Hanson, one of the bomb squad people starts yelling:

"EVERYONE BACK – BACK TO THE OTHER SIDE OF THE ROAD!"

Our trio immediately responds to his command. Both officers trot over to our new location.

"Are you Mr. Riggs?" one of the men asks.

"That's me."

"Lieutenant Campfield, Franklin County Sheriff's Department."

We shake hands. I hate shaking hands.

"Well Mr. Riggs, I don't quite know how you knew there was a bomb in there..."

"Is there one in there?"

"Ohh yeah. A half pound of C4 planted underneath your seat."

"I KNEW IT!"

"The device is pretty crude but from what we can see, it's set up to detonate at a certain pressure."

"What kind of pressure?"

"The kind created by your ass when you sit down."

"Oh, that kind."

"We'll have our detonating team here in about an hour. Do you have any idea who's responsible for this?"

Agent Outlaw jumps in.

"Yes Lieutenant, we do. I'm with the FBI and we have a suspect or two we're looking at."

"So we don't have to investigate this?"

"Nope, if you'll just disarm it and have one of your crime scene people dust for prints, we'll take it from here."

"That's good news. Budget cuts and all you know."

Both deputies walk away with the look of relief on their faces. I check my cell phone and it's now three o'clock. It's probably shift change and no one in this business wants to work overtime. The job is difficult enough.

"So Marvin – what's this about your father?"

"Mark, I promise I'll tell you but later. I'm not in the mood right now."

I glare into the eyes of Agent Outlaw who now knows I'm pissed.

"Sorry Marvin, I just assumed he knew."

"Don't worry about it. If anyone has the right to know the truth, it's him. Oh, by the way, I almost forgot."

I reach into my pocket and pull out the copy of the application and hand it to Outlaw.

"What's this?"

"It's a copy of an application submitted by John Merrick when he attended a woodworking class at Wilson College in Thiensville."

"Who's John Merrick?" Hanson asks.

"It's part of the father story I'm going to tell you later."

"Check the name of the reference he listed as his uncle on the bottom."

"Both Hanson and Outlaw scan the bottom of the application and simultaneously look at one another."

"Did you see it? It says Dr. Joseph Winger. It has to be the same medical examiner in town. He even lists his address as Bedford."

"Yeah, we see it Marvin."

"So we need to talk to this guy, and now. I know for a fact that in his desk drawer, he has a file with John Merrick's name listed on the tab."

"How do you know that?" Outlaw asks.

"Don't worry how I know – I just do. This man knows something. I would normally talk to the guy myself but since I've got you involved, I want to have you both there as a witness."

Hanson clears his throat.

"We're not going to be able to talk to him Marvin."

"Why not?"

"Because we just identified him as the body we found in your apartment."

CHAPTER 29

It's four-thirty and I'm finally on the road heading for home. As I make my left onto a narrow back road, the word "home" is running through my mind over and over. I say I'm heading home but I really don't have one. I begin to ask myself; what is home? Is it four walls and a roof, or is it even a place at all? I then remember how I felt back at the archery range a few hours ago. There are no walls, no bathrooms, no fancy knick-knacks hanging around. So I guess home is nothing more than familiarity. Feeling comfortable in a place where pleasant memories surround you. Come to think of it; I feel at home right now in my car.

I travel a few miles down Williamson Road in an attempt to get onto the freeway and back to Bedford. I'm in no hurry. I don't even know what I'm going to do when I get there. I take that back – I know what I'm going to do. I'm going to find who's responsible for all of this. Who out there wants me dead? It's time to start some serious digging for some answers. They've made it very clear they don't care how I die. I think it's time that I return the favor.

I arrive at a stretch of asphalt that is unusually flat. The hilly terrain doesn't allow many stretches of road like this. It gives me the opportunity to look ahead for a change – and I do.

To my surprise, I see a car up ahead. The taillights signify a Ford Crown Victoria – black; just like the one those two goons were in. Could it be?

I floor the accelerator, reaching a speed of seventy and pushing for more. In no time, I'm on the back bumper of the Crown Victoria. The windows are slightly tinted and I can just make out the outline of one person in the car – the driver. There's no way of telling if it's who I think it is. It could be some old man who lives back here. I'll need to be cautious.

I begin to follow the car at a normal speed. While doing so, I reach over to the glove box and retrieve my service revolver. With one hand I chamber a round. It's now apparent that I'll kill if I have to. If this is who I hope it's not, then God help him. Force is the only thing that gets these peoples attention. They have no sense of right or wrong, no compassion; Nothing. All they know is to get the job done. I'm sick and tired of being pushed around. I will not be anyone's completed task.

The black vehicle stops at a four-way intersection. The area is very secluded with no homes or people around that I can see. The man is still stopped and is now looking in his review mirror back at me. I still can't be sure it's him. I'll need to be patient. There are enough innocent people being killed in the world already. I don't plan on adding to that number.

After a few seconds of waiting, I am starting to get nervous. Something is not right here. I've spooked whoever is driving this car. Just then, the driver's door opens and out steps my pursuer. The son-of-a-bitch back at the archery range is standing at his door with a smirk on his face, daring me to do something. He had his chance, and so did I. If I had it to do all over again, I'd put an "Easton" carbonate filled arrow with a steel tip right in his gut. I would have made sure that the arrow hit him dead center as to split his spinal cord in half so he would lie there and suffer from his paralyzed state. This would have allowed me to possibly extract some much needed information before killing him. I say possibly because guys like these normally don't talk. They are paid to keep their mouths shut. I'm about to get a second chance at him. Let's see if I can't shut him up for good.

From first gear, I slide the shifter into reverse and slowly back up a few yards. He's still standing there. He thinks I'm afraid of him. I was at one time. Not anymore. He's about to get a big surprise: A genuine wake-up call.

With enough distance between him and me for a running start, I put the shifter in first gear, dump the clutch, and hit the gas. I accelerate quickly as the front end of my car speeds towards him. He's no longer smirking. I watch as he realizes what I'm about to do and attempts to protect himself by getting back into his car. I ram his car at forty miles per hour and nail him square in the driver's door. I watch as he flies backwards with a look of shock on his face. But he's a professional at what he does and soon starts firing round after round from the passenger's side of his damaged vehicle. I anticipate it and exit my vehicle with my head down and my weapon already in-hand. I blindly fire rounds back at my pursuer with no precision what-so-ever.

"YOU'RE A DEAD MAN RIGGS," I hear being yelled in my direction.

I say nothing. I'm looking for any edge I can get. I lift my head and peek through the broken glass window. I can see him trying to open his passenger's side door while keeping an eye on me. He sees me and starts firing again. Two more rounds soar over my head. I then get an idea – a great idea, but I'm not sure it'll work. It's something I saw on TV once.

I remove my ball cap and ease over to the front of my vehicle. I can still hear him cursing and swearing at me. I lift my hat just high enough so he can see it. My plan works. He starts firing at the hat thinking it's my head underneath. Not so. I'm standing a few feet to the left and quickly stand upright. With his concentration on the hat, I get a bead on his chest and fire all six rounds into him. Each one making a thud sound as it enters his body. He jerks backwards with each round making contact. I stop firing when he is out of my sight. No more rounds are flying my way.

I look up and down the road and still not a car in sight. I ease my head up again and see my pursuer sucking the last bit of life he can. With the swagger of Clint Eastwood after smoking that dude on the peer, I walk over to his vehicle and open the passenger's side door. The body rolls out and falls to the shoulder of the road. I stand over him and stare as his cold dead eyes look back at me.

"Now how's my shoot'n asshole?"

After a minute to collect my thoughts, I begin the tasks of going through this dead man's pockets to get some idea of who he is. Just as I thought, there is none. No driver's license, no credit cards, absolutely nothing. I did find a money clip with three-hundred dollars inside. Since he's not going to need that anytime soon, I'll put it to good use.

But now I have a problem. What am I going to do with the mess I made? I can't just leave it. The authorities will eventually be notified by a passing motorist and when they run my tag, I'll be answering more questions. I'm tired of answering questions I don't have answers to.

After some thought, I realize where I am at. The cross street I'm at is named 'Quarry Road'. Quarry as in 'a deep hole.' The quarry is only thirty yards to my left. I suddenly get an idea. I run back to my car and get in. I turn the key in the ignition with my fingers crossed, and it starts.

"YES!"

I back my car up a few feet and exit. I walk around to the passenger's side and, with a few tugs, I'm able to pull the front fender off the tire. Smoke is steaming out of the radiator but I'm not concerned. I just need the car to run only a minute more. I then walk to the far side of the dead man's car and load him back inside, making sure to tie him down with a seat belt. Before closing the door, I reach over and put the Crown Victoria into neutral. I also take the time to turn the front wheels on this boat in the direction of the quarry.

I get back into my car and maneuver behind the Ford. With assistance from my front bumper, I begin pushing the Ford across the intersection and straight for the quarry. After getting the car rolling, I smash the accelerator and catapult his car straight into the ditch. It disappears as I hit the brakes and exit. I run to the shoulder and watch as the car clears the ditch and does a swan dive right into the water.

The car floats like a bobber in the water at first, but soon sinks after water fills the interior through the smashed-out windows. My plan works. By the time they find him and his car in this seventy-five feet deep quarry, I'll be an elderly gent at the old-folks home eating pureed beef and getting beat at checkers by my grandchildren.

CHAPTER 30

My three mile walk into town took about an hour. I now have a window seat in aisle five on this surprisingly nice Greyhound bus; thanks to my dead friend who was kind enough to loan me three hundred bucks. It's five-thirty and the nice lady at the counter said I would be in Bedford by nine. The manifest on the wall at the bus stop indicated twenty-one stops between here and there. The good thing is I don't have to change buses. Be a good time to think about my next move. I'm sure I've got more than one to make.

My first thought is that of my car. Back at the scene of the crime I didn't have many options. Now that I am a murderer (so to speak), I couldn't just leave it there for the cops to find. And I couldn't tow it back to Bedford in that condition. They would ask too many questions. I'm tired of questions. I'm tired of talking all together.

So my car is now at the bottom of the quarry, with hopes of never being seen again. I thought best that it disappear along with my dead friend. I did retrieve a few things from it first. A few pictures of my girls, my Dale Earnhardt ball cap with a new bullet hole in it, and my gun. I've got three rounds left. I'll need to get some more. I still don't know how many more I'm going to have to kill before this all ends. I anticipate two more - the partner that was with the quarry guy and whoever hired these goons. It doesn't really matter. I'm no longer playing the victim they want me to. I'm done with this game. Done!

I then remember what Outlaw told me back at the range. They found Dr. Winger dead in my apartment. Makes about as much sense as a penny costing two cents to make. He was looking for something. I can only assume it was either the diamond or information on my father. I know the answer to both of those. Outlaw has the diamond and Dad's in the deep freeze. It's too bad I had to answer my cell when Mandi called yesterday. It would have been a real advantage to be dead right now. I could sneak around and really do some digging. But that chance has come and gone so I'll have to play the hand I've been dealt.

I think about Mandi a lot. I haven't seen her in awhile. I do miss the life we had prior to all of this. I retrieve my cell and hit the designated speed-dial. The phone rings only once.

"Marvin?"

"Hi Mandi."

"Where are you?"

"I'll be in Bedford at nine. Could you possibly pick me up at the bus stop?"

"THE BUS STOP?"

"Yeah, I had some car trouble."

"What kind of trouble?

"Some guy pulled out in front of me on the way back from the archery range."

"Is the other guy okay?"

"He died."

"Oh Marvin, quit kidding around."

"Well if you knew the answer, why'd you ask the question?"

"I'll be there at nine. Is it the one on Riley Road?"

"That's the one. Thanks Babe."

"See you there."

The call ends quickly and with not much fanfare. I can tell she's somewhat reluctant to resume our relationship to the standards I have become accustomed to. I guess if the roles were reversed, I'd feel the same way. And at this point there's no way I can put in the time and energy required to make it work.

I lean back in the comfortable bus seat and close my eyes. I'm so tired. My day started early this morning. Thought I'd have a relaxing day at the range but like most of my plans lately, they never seem to pan out.

I check my cell and find that an hour has passed since boarding this bus. I've been in and out of consciousness trying to grab a nap between stops. A new stop is coming up. The bus driver announces that we're in Newburg. It's dark now and difficult to see outside. The air brakes activate once again and the bus comes to another stop. I look out through the tinted glass and see no bus stop, just a small, older residential area filled with homes for the working class; folks who have to ride a bus to and from work in order to keep food on the table and a roof over their heads.

I watch as a number of folks stand and shuffle their way toward the front and out the only exit available. It was then I saw him. It was a man whose face looked eerily familiar to me. It causes me to jolt in my seat. The image so familiar that it forces me to retrieve the only picture I have tucked in my coat pocket. I quickly scan the photo and then at the man who caught my attention. It's him – John Merrick.

"It's impossible" I mutter under my breath.

I look again and the resemblance is remarkable. I instantly exit my seat and follow the man off the bus. Without thinking about where I'm at or how I would get home, I begin walking down the side walk behind the man, keeping a distance in order to figure out what I'm going to do here. One thing is for sure, I'm not getting back on the bus. It just left.

As I follow the man, I can't help but wonder if this is truly him. I never actually saw the body the night he was shot. I was going on information that was given to me. My dad told me who it was. He would have no reason to lie. Then again, he lied about selling at least one of those diamonds. And what am I going to say to this guy. Excuse me sir, are you John Merrick – the dead guy?

I decide to wing it as I do with most things in my life. I jog up behind the man, which catches his attention. He turns around to face me as if he was about to be attacked.

"Excuse me sir, I mean you no harm what's so ever."

"Can I help you?" He says.

"Would your name happen to be John Merrick?"

A look of concern and puzzlement invades the man's face. I struck a nerve with my question. The street lights are bad but there's enough light to read the name tag sewed into this work shirt: KASS.

"Why do you ask?"

"Boy if I had a week, I could probably explain it to you – but I don't."

"Did you know my brother?"

"Brother?"

The man pauses for a few seconds and takes a deep breath.

"John Merrick is my twin brother. Did you know him?"

"I met him briefly.

"HE'S ALIVE?" the man yells.

"I don't know. This was two years ago. My father was a woodshop instructor at a college in Chambersburg. John was one of his students."

"Oh, so you thought I was him."

"Yes."

"Our family hasn't seen John in over ten years. We just assumed…."

"Assumed what?"

"You ask too many questions mister. By the way, what is your name?"

"Marvin Riggs."

The man stares at me longer than I like.

"You're the guy on TV that killed those hunters up on the mountain."

I chuckle

"You think that's funny?" he asks.

"No I don't. What is funny is that everyone just assumes I'm guilty just because someone on TV said I was. Why do you think John hasn't been seen for so many years?"

"Good day, Mr. Riggs."

"Excuse me. This is very important. Why won't you tell me?"

"Because I am not at liberty to discuss it."

"Okay, then who is?"

"I would suggest you contact the FBI first, or if you can, find a guy by the last name of Winger. He'll be able to tell ya."

"Joseph Winger? Dr. Joseph Winger?"

"You know him?"

"I did, until he was blown up."

"I'm not surprised. And I wouldn't be shocked if my brother has met with the same fate."

"Why do you say that?"

"Contact the FBI Mr. Riggs. They'll have the answers you're looking for."

The man turns and heads down the street, not looking back to see if I'll follow him. I have no reason to. I find myself upset that I didn't get more information but also feeling very fortunate that I even ran into this man. What are the odds? I need to get back to Bedford. Outlaw should be able to give me some answers. But I must first obtain some ammunition. I'm not entering town without a loaded piece of hardware. I saw a pawn shop a few blocks back that advertised ammunition for sale on their store window. I also need to pick up a holster as well. My piece is killing my back.

CHAPTER 31

Two blocks north of the bus stop is the pawn shop I saw earlier. I'm standing in front of it now. Al's Pawn Shop is what the large wooden sign reads. Too bad Al doesn't collect paint and brushes, because this place needs a good coat or two. If I had to guess, I would say this building was erected sometime during the 1930's. The detail in the molding is incredible.

I open the wooden door to the shop. As I enter, I get a sense of going back in time. Like a time machine, I see fifty years disappear in the blink of an eye. The stale smell of cigar smoke is in the air. It's a smell that would normally irritate me. But in this old building, the smell is sweet and somewhat aromatic. It belongs here, along with the mold, dust balls, and the old man behind the counter who is currently staring at me over the top of his bifocals.

"What can I do for ya young man?" he asks in a low, shattered voice.

"Need some ammo and I do appreciate the young man comment."

"Everyone who's upright is younger than I am. Guess how old I am?"

The frail human being hunched over before me with a cigar in his hand has to be over ninety. If I had to guess, I would say he goes no more than eighty pounds soaking wet. Every muscle that consumes his body is pointing south and swaying to the beat of his Parkinson's disease as he maneuvers around the counter. Gravity has been pulling at his face as well and for a long time. His mouth barely moves as he speaks. And that droll hanging from the corner of his mouth will probably be there until his next meal, but he has no idea of its existence.

"I would say you're about seventy eight."

"I'm ninety five and still vertical. What kind of ammo are you looking for?"

"Need some .357 rounds. Got any?"

"Got a few left. $8.95 for a box of twenty."

"I just need one."

"Hollow points or standard load?"

"Hollow points will do me just fine."

The old man shuffles around and opens an unlocked safe behind him. The safe is taller than he is and probably just as old. I can't help but wonder what good a safe is if you leave it open. As quickly as he possibly can, he secures a box of the much needed ammunition while I pull out my piece from my waistband. I want to make sure these rounds fit before I take them with me. It's a habit I developed from my father in the early years of my hunting career. I think it's the ass-whoop'n I got that stays with me.

I was no more than thirteen years old at the time when my father decided to do some ruff grouse hunting. For reasons I don't recall, I did not attend the hunt on that Saturday in October, so my recollection of this event comes to me via third party.

The ruff grouse is the official state bird of Pennsylvania. It's about the size of an overweight pigeon that dons light and dark brown feathers.

What makes this bird such a challenge for hunters is its incredible speed. You know it's a grouse when you hear the thumping sound they make while they fly. This bird (for some reason) likes to take its wings and thump its chest. It makes a sound comparable to a bongo drum.

My Dad was hunting an area called Siding Hill in Huntington County, known for its good population of grouse. He was sitting comfortably against a large oak tree when the impossible happened. A ruff grouse flew in and landed fifteen yards in front of him. According to Dad, he was amazed at his good fortune as he steadied his 12-gauge shotgun on the elusive bird.

Now like I said before, I wasn't there, so don't shoot the messenger.

My dad took aim and pulled the trigger with all expectations of telling his buddies of his incredible luck – NOT! The instant the trigger was pulled, he knew something wasn't right. The standard bang from the firing pin striking the primer and catapulting the wad of buckshot toward the intended target was nothing more than a thump; like that of the bird he was trying to harvest. Then the wad of buckshot that was suppose to exit the barrel of the shotgun faster than the human eye can see, just rolled out the end of the gun barrel and fell to the ground.

The grouse reportedly looked up at Dad, said a Hail Mary, and flew off, never to be seen again. My dad opened the action to the gun to determine what just happened. The spent shotgun shell casing flew out and the problem was quickly identified. My father owned a 12-gauge shotgun, while I owned a 16-gauge. Being a teenager and not paying attention to detail like I do now, I had accidentally placed my box of 16-gauge shells in dad's part of the gun cabinet. So when he grabbed a box of shells that morning, he had no reason to check and see if they were the correct ones. I won't go into detail about what happened when he got home; let's just say I never made that mistake again.

So from that day on, I have always checked to make sure that I

had the correct ammunition for whatever type or caliber weapon I was
using on that particular day.

"HEY, WHAT ARE YOU DOING?" the old man barks out
loud.

"What?"

"You can't bring a gun in here."

"Sure I can – I just did."

"Can't you read boy. The sign out front says no guns inside."

"What's your name sir?"

"AL."

"Okay AL. First of all, I am a game warden and this is my service
weapon. And secondly, I'm not going to rob you or anything. I just
want to make sure these rounds fit."

"Hey I know you. You're that game warden fellow that killed those
people up on the mountain, aren't you?"

"Well obviously you've been watching too much television. If I was
one responsible, don't you think I'd be in jail?"

"You might be on the run."

"Yeah that its, I'm on the run – eluding the police. How much will
it be for the shells?"

"It'll be $9.45 with tax."

"I also need a holster; something simple I can carry this hunk of
steel on my belt. I like that one hanging up behind you."

The old geezer shuffles around and retrieves my request. He then
flings the holster at me in an attempt to show whose boss around here.
I smile at the old guy and admire his toughness. The holster is perfect
and I fling a fifty dollar bill on the counter to show my approval.

"Keep the change old man. And if you say anything to anyone that
I was here, you and I will be meeting again. Are we clear?"

"Crystal."

"You have a nice evening."

I load my gun and holster and make my way out of the store. I probably shouldn't have done that – pick on the old guy like that. The shop looked like it held some real treasures and I would have loved to stick around and see what all he had. But he believes that I'm guilty just because he saw it on television. Don't feel much like hanging around and being accused of something I didn't do. One would think that by this time, I'd be used to it.

I grab the next bus forty-five minutes later. In lieu of sitting inside the bus shelter, I plant my rear end across the street in between two bushes that appear harmless in the dark. It wasn't until I got halfway in that the thorns began to make themselves known. I sucked it up and had a seat anyways. I don't trust the old man at the pawn shop. He was just cagey enough to call the police on me, so I decide to stay out of sight until the bus arrives. I do not want any cops around me right now. I want no questions asked of me or interruptions taking place. Before this is all over, more are going to die; and more than likely I'll be doing the killing. No more cops.

While I wait, I call Mandi and tell her that I'm running behind. Of course, she wanted an explanation and I gave her one. It wasn't the truth but she didn't say she wanted the actual explanation – just an explanation. She begins a rant that lasts a few minutes. Telling me how irresponsible I am and how I need to get my shit together. I just laid the phone down and let her go. When I stopped hearing nagging and bitching, I picked it back up and apologized. But it was too late; she had already hung-up on me.

I have a theory about women and that nagging thing they do. I believe it is their way of relieving stress. Men are told at a very young age to maintain and to deal with it. My dad used to tell me to 'suck it up' all the time. So guys internalize everything, which is the reason most of your spree killers are men. They just blow a gasket all at once and start shoot'n. Women, however, get it out by talking. It is their way of venting. And the more we as men resist that, the more we're going to have to listen to. It's the one reason men fart more than women - they can never generate the required pressure.

CHAPTER 32

After about forty-five minutes of walking from the bus stop on a cold November evening, I find myself standing at the far north side of Mandi's apartment complex. I dressed for the weather so the cold is not a problem. In fact I'm dressed too well. I'm sweating like a Russian race horse. I have no idea what that means. Dad used to say it all the time. I can only assume race horses in Russia perspire more than others.

I scan the lot and not a creature is stirring. I look at apartment #10 and Mandi's already left for work. There's not a light on inside anywhere. Her car is also missing, which assures me that I can gain access without being detected. That's important when you're not invited in.

I run to the door with key in hand. This is the same key she gave me months ago when we decided to start dating. I insert the key the moment I reach the door, praying to God that it works. I need food, a shower, and some Internet access really bad. I turn the key.

"Yes!"

I enter quickly and lock the door behind me. I've been here before – many times before, so I know the layout. I walk through the small kitchen and straight to the computer located in the far corner of the living room. I hit the power button and the light from the monitor illuminates the entire room. I would prefer no lights but not much I can do about it. I don't anticipate this taking long.

After all the virus software does their job, I finally get on Google. I stop for a moment and think about what it is I need to find out. That question is obvious: Who is setting me up? But where do I start. I can't just type in the search field, 'Who is setting up Marvin Riggs.' If it were that easy, I'd a run a search after they called my ass in to interrogate me.

I decide to begin with what I know. I know that Joseph Winger was found dead in my apartment. But then again, do I? I'm just going on what Outlaw told me. I wasn't there. Hell, I don't even know if they even found a body. I do know one thing for sure. Winger had a file in his desk drawer labeled with the name of John Merrick. In that file was his picture. Winger is the key to learning the truth.

I type his name into the search field and quickly get a list of possible hits. I have a preconceived notion that this guy would be all over the World Wide Web. Folks in the medical field normally like themselves more than that rest of us do. I guess ten years of schooling would make anyone a little pompous. And most of these folks like to write about their area of expertise, which always seems to land on the Internet. Anything and everything you need to know from moles to mopeds can be found at the click of a button.

As I run down the list of sights that Google has provided me, I'm unable to find anything on Winger. It's hard to believe but it's true. Anyone with a Ph.D in this country must have written something in a medical journal or publication. Most educated folks (like doctors) have huge egos and feel the need be at the forefront of whatever they do.

I stop to reflect. I know that Winger is from this area. In fact, Merrick is as well. Maybe the newspapers have something. Maybe somebody did a story on him once. Folks who become physicians around here are rare. This is blue-collar county and ninety-five percent of the population here works for a living. They use their hands, not their brains to carve out a life.

I do a search for newspapers in the area and my efforts find nothing. That's not to say there's not a local paper here, just none online. I check the nearby town of Cumberland in the State of Maryland. I find the Cumberland Times online and ready to assist me with a section for archiving records from many years ago. I rub my hands together in celebration, as if I just found out my ex-wife is getting remarried. No more alimony payments.

I click on the link and type Winger's name in the search field. Immediately I get notification that there are four articles in archive for him. I'm also notified it will cost me $9.95 to view them.

After inputting my debt card information for all those unemployed computer geeks to steal, I click the first article and find a brief story about the graduation class of 1970 from Bedford High school. Winger's name is mentioned due to the fact he finished number one in his class. His major course of study was science; which makes perfect sense.

The rest of the article is a list of names of students who finished high school with a variety of honors. It takes me back to my graduation. I know I was there because I recall wearing this blue silky gown. And I remember the feeling of freedom when the ceremony concluded. The fact that I never had to sit in a classroom ever again was one of the best moments of my life. These poor kids now-a-days who finish high school are just beginning. Without a college degree in this country, one would have a difficult time apply for a job in their local sanitation department. Thank God it's not my problem anymore.

I click off the article and check out the next one. It was a repeat of the first – word for word. I immediately go to the third and find an article with a photo this time. Joseph Winger is standing proudly along side another gentleman in their cap and gown, holding their college diplomas in their hands. I briefly look at the second gentleman but didn't pay him much attention until I read the name: John Kass.

"KASS!"

It's the same name on the guy's shirt I confronted outside the bus stop. Kass wasn't his first name – it was his last. He knew Winger because he graduated from college with him. The next paragraph causes me even more stress – more questions that'll need to be answered.

Bedford's own Joseph Winger and John Kass stand in front of their dorm room at Penn State University with diplomas in-hand. Both graduated this week with degrees in criminal justice and will be entering the FBI academy together in July.

"FBI?"

CHAPTER 33

It's eight o'clock in the morning and I'm sitting in the lobby of the FBI building waiting on Outlaw to arrive. After a shower and a descent night's sleep at Mandi's place, I rode my bike over here to play on a hunch, based on the article I read last night. Both Winger and Kass went to the academy. One can assume that both then worked for the FBI. Why in the world would anyone go through all that and not become an agent? What puzzles me is why Winger turned out to be a medical examiner and Kass, a homeless man living out of a motor home. It doesn't make any sense. And then I remember something Outlaw said to me while I was being interrogated. He mentioned the note found on the diamond that indicated John Merrick as the reason behind all of this. He showed me the diamond but not the note. Why? He said Merrick's name with such confidence, that it bothered me then and still does. It was like he knew – like he had knowledge of something. I have a feeling he's holding something back. Serves me right. I was holding back on him as well.

It's eight twelve when Outlaw enters the building and sees me sitting.

"Marvin, what are you doing here?"

"Wait'n on you."

"Everything okay?"

"I guess – you got a few minutes?"

"Sure, come on back."

A few security checks and a brief walk down the hallway later, we're in Outlaw's office and I take a seat without permission. Outlaw does the same.

"So what's up, Marvin."

"Tell me about Winger? What do you know about him?"

"Not much. I know he started working here as the medical examiner about two years ago. He came highly recommended."

"By who?"

"I'm not sure. It's just what I heard."

"Did you know he attended the FBI academy in Virginia after graduating from college?"

Outlaw hesitates with his answer.

"Yes"

"Why did you pause before answering that one?"

"I have my reasons. Why are you asking?"

"Did you know that he attended the academy with a college buddy of his by the name of Kass?"

Outlaw's face becomes blank. He stares at me briefly and then at the ceiling. He quickly ejects himself from his seat and closes his office door. He takes a seat beside me and lowers his voice.

"What do you know about Kass, Marvin?"

"So there is something up."

"What is it you know Marvin?"

"I know that both Kass and Winger attended the academy but they weren't on the list of cadets who graduated that year. I also know that Kass has a twin brother who lives in Newburg. And that being the case,

John Merrick is not John Merrick. What I don't know is who was killed in my dad's shop that evening."

"You know Riggs sometimes you just shouldn't stick your nose in things that don't concern you."

"Oh, so now it's Riggs. And by the way, you stick that finger in my face one more time, you're gonna lose it."

Outlaw backs off.

"Okay, I'll make a deal with you. You tell me everything I want to know about your dad and I'll tell you everything you want to know about Winger and Kass. And you go first - deal?"

"Deal."

Outlaw returns to his seat behind the desk and leans back in his chair. He picks up the phone and advises the switchboard operator that he is not available for calls.

"Okay Marvin first question. Where's your father at right now?"

"After the fiasco in Wisconsin, he moved up to the mountains."

"What mountains?"

"Up on Martin's Hill."

"You mean he's here?"

"He was."

"What does that mean?"

I pause to collect myself.

"He built a cabin up on the mountain and was living there for the past two years. You remember the call I got the last time we spoke here?"

"Yeah"

"That was my brother. He found the old man dead of what we think was a heart attack in his easy chair."

"No shit. Are you sure it was heart failure?"

"We don't know. He didn't have a mark on him so we ruled out any foul play. It's not like we could call the coroner and the authorities. To the world, this man was dead."

"Do you know how much trouble you could be in for this."

"I know. Why do you think we kept it such a secret? Wouldn't you do the same for your old man?"

"Nope" says Outlaw without hesitation."

"Why not?"

"You'll find out in a minute. One more question. What did you do with his body? I know you didn't bury it, not up here with the ground already frozen."

"He's preserved."

"Where?"

"We put him in his freezer up at the cabin."

"Shut up"

"We did. I swear to God. We didn't know what else to do at the time. I figured we'd bury him in the spring."

"I want to go up to the cabin after we're done here."

"That depends on how good your information is."

"Oh mine's good – trust me."

"Okay. Your turn. I want to know who died in my dad's shop."

"The man's name was John Kass. He is the twin brother of Jeff Kass who somehow you ran into in Newburg. And you're right; Winger and Kass did attend the academy together. They were standouts and caught the attention of the bureau. They were both pulled prior to graduation and assigned to an office together. Those two were inseparable."

"What office were they assigned to?"

"The one over in Fredrick. Rumor has it that a few months into their tenure, their relationship went south. Kass had a daughter that caught the roving eye of Winger. The two started dating even though Winger was married and many years her senior. This went on for a few months until one night, when Kass caught them together and went ballistic. A fight ensued, which ended when Kass' head made contact with a lead pipe. Kass suffered brain damage from the attack and Winger was thrown out of the bureau."

"So that's why Winger's career as an agent ended so abruptly. I can't believe he got a job as a medical examiner with a criminal record."

"He was never charged with a crime Marvin."

"How does that happen?"

"I'm not sure. I suspect the bureau didn't want the attention of the media. It's believed that both of them were working some top level stuff. Any media coverage of such an incident would jeopardize any undercover operations they would be working on."

"I can see their point. So we know where Winger ended up in life – what about Kass."

"He remained with the bureau."

"He did? What would a guy with brain damage do for the bureau?"

"He wasn't as damaged as he led on. From what I know, he used that to gain access into some tough cases. He worked mostly drugs and smuggling cases, organizations that were tough to penetrate."

"You don't think he was watching my dad, do ya?"

Outlaw pauses, leans over, and points his finger in my face like a child who just got catch stealing."

"Marvin, you keep this to yourself or I swear.."

"He was watching dad, wasn't he?"

"Kass was working a smuggling case when he met your father. The bureau was onto your father transporting those deer back from the coast. Kass was assigned to keep a close eye on him. He played the retard act and made your dad believe he was this poor homeless guy who just needed a friend."

"So they knew my dad was alive."

"Yes they did. Do you really believe that they didn't know who was lying dead in your dad's shop?" They knew who it was that night. When you go that deep undercover, it's like working for the CIA; you just eventually vanish. Then your dad disappeared and the bureau eventually gave up on the case."

"Well someone didn't give up on it."

"That's apparent."

"Holy Shit! All of this over some part-time job."

"Yeap, and the sad part about it is, your father and those drivers were all innocent."

"Whatever became of the daughter?"

"Don't know. I don't even know her name. You gotta understand what I've just told you is what I've learned second hand and through some reports I've read."

"So someone who knows about all of this is trying to keep this quiet by having me locked up for murder. That doesn't make any sense. Why don't they just kill me?"

"They've tried."

"Yeah, but not until lately. I'll bet you whoever is behind this thought they would just lock me up and that would be it. When they didn't, they went to the next level."

"That's possible."

"So Winger must have been involved in this somehow. He was snooping around my apartment when the bomb went off. That means whoever he was working with screwed up or turned on him."

"So when do you want to head up to the cabin Marvin?"

"Not right now; give me a day. I need to think about all of this and also contact my brother."

"Why your brother?"

"Because he is the other person who knows my dad didn't die two years ago. If they're trying to shut me up, I'm sure he'll be next."

CHAPTER 34

Grissom Park is one of my favorite hiding spots. It's a beautiful one-acre spread filed with trees and wildlife for everyone to enjoy. At the far end of the park is where all the swing sets and climbing devices are situated adjacent to the ball field.

During the summer months in my twenties, I would often sit in the bleachers and reminisce about my playing days; wondering what could have been if I would have only taken the game more seriously. Would I have been good enough to go to the major leagues? But at the time, it was nothing more than a game to me.

I remember standing inside the batters box waiting on the pitch to come in. With my eyes closed, I would take a big hack at anything that was within ten feet of me. I was always afraid of being hit by the ball. My fear was justified though.

I was about twelve years old when one evening I approached the plate to take yet another stab at anything thrown my way. Before entering the box, I made the required look over at the third base coach. To my surprise, he gave me the bunt sign. Looking back now, it made perfect sense. We had a base runner on first and only one out. It was late in the game and we were only up by one run. The plan was to get the runner over to second and into scoring position.

I enter the batters box and my nerves were in high gear. I stared down the pitcher as he made his wind-up and I didn't let on to my attentions until the very last second. The delivery was made and I quickly squared to bunt.

Now when one bunts a ball, the object is to let the ball strike the barrel of the bat without swinging. I did all the above except for one thing: I failed to remove my hand from the barrel of the bat and I bunted the ball off my left middle finger. The instantaneous surge of pain was incredible and the amount of blood loss would make one think that I had just been shot.

In spite of all this, the ball rolled perfectly onto the playing field and I took off running. Each stride increased the pain and I found myself jumping, crying, and running all at the same time.

Unbeknownst to me at the time, my spectacle caught the opposing team off-guard. According to witnesses at the scene, they just stared at me as I hopped from base to base like a redneck with a butt-crack full of fire ants.

I made it to second base before they even attempted a throw, which was way off the mark. I just remember looking at my third base coach who told me to keeping running.

The play ended with me scoring a triple on a bunt and scoring the runner. It's probably the only bunt triple in baseball's recorded history. I was a hero that day and remember nothing but the pain. I do remember the trip to the doctor's office and him sticking a hot needle in my fingernail to relieve the pressure.

But I'm not at the ball field today. Life is not as carefree for me anymore. Those days are gone. I'm at the other side of the park, backed into a wooded area. I often sit here to get away from the world and collect my thoughts. I have lots of those lately.

My cell phone says it's eleven o'clock and my stomach says it's time for lunch. I've been sitting here for two hours trying to get a handle of what is happening, and not making much progress. I think about Winger and what he could have been looking for in my apartment. He was involved in this from the beginning. He could have been looking for evidence on the whereabouts of my father. But what would he care? He hated Kass. If anything he would have sent me flowers for getting rid of him. That way, he and the daughter could continue their relationship.

I start the car and pull out onto the road, with intentions of hitting Taco Bell this morning. Kind of in the mood for a one of those grilled stuffed burritos and a tall Coca-Cola. As I make my way into the city, I wonder if the daughter will be attending Winger's funeral. I sure would like to talk with her. I'll bet my bottom dollar she'd have some information that could bust this thing wide open.

I soon arrive at Taco Bell and wait behind a few cars already sitting in the drive thru. I thought sure I'd be the first one here today but no such luck. I'm not a regular here at Taco Hell but I'm so Subway'd out. A man can only consume so many foot-longs.

I lean back in my seat and stare at the six-foot tall menu in front of me. I quickly decide I'll need to tell the person trapped inside the speaker box making a minimum wage that I'll have a number six. I'm sure I'll have to repeat it several times but I've got all day, or so I think.

I look over to my right and see a payphone. It jogs my memory that this is the same payphone where our suspect called in those deaths. The same one Mandi and I found a few weeks ago. As I stare at it, movement from the adjacent building catches my attention. I look up toward the corner eave and see something that makes my heart race - something I've been looking for ever since this bullshit started. The possible break I've been looking for – A SECURITY CAMERA!

CHAPTER 35

All of a sudden, my appetite is gone. The sight of the surveillance camera attached to the corner of the adjacent building has satisfied my hunger. It wasn't just the camera that filled me up – it was where they mounted it.

Lucky enough to have no one behind me, I back out of the drive thru and into the parking lot of the Cigarette Depot. I quickly exit my vehicle and stare at the monitoring device. I watch the camera pan back and forth directly into the path of the payphone. It's the same phone used to notify us of the dead bodies on the mountain. Could I have missed this when I was here a few weeks ago with Mandi? For God sake, I haven't lost my touch yet – have I? I'm only forty-seven and I thought I was still as sharp as a tack. It then occurs to me that they may have put that camera up since then and I'm just wasting my time. There's only one way to find out.

I enter the 24/7 establishment for the very first time. I scamper to the counter and startle the clerk, who is probably used to folks looking around first before arriving at the register.

"Can I help you?" she asks in a three pack-a-day voice.

"I sure hope so. Can you tell me how long your security camera has been mounted at the corner of your building?"

The woman who appears to be in her fifties and has never met a pizza she didn't like, stares at me with a look of confusion.

"Why do you want to know that?"

"Well, I work for the Games Commission here in town and we are working…"

"Wait a second. I know you. You're that guy who killed those hunters on top of the mountain."

Here we go again.

"Ma'am, I did not kill anyone. We are still investigating the case. Do you think that if I were responsible for those heinous acts that I'd be here talking to you right now?

She stares once again, trying to make sense of what I just said. I can tell she's having difficulty with it. I give her no chance to respond.

"Ma'am, we really need your help. What if I told you…well, maybe I shouldn't."

"What?"

I pause.

"What's your name ma'am?"

"Alice"

"Okay Alice, here's the deal."

I quickly pan the store and find that we are alone.

"That camera maybe the key to solving this case."

"Really?"

"Yes. How long has it been there?"

"We put it up last year after the third robbery. The goons were parking behind the store. I would never see them coming."

"Alice, what I'm about to tell you is not to be repeated. Can you keep a secret?"

"You bet!"

"You know that payphone over at Taco Bell?"

"Yeah"

"That was the phone where someone called in to report the first two deaths of those hunters."

"Really."

Alice pauses for a moment. She looks up at the stained ceiling tiles looking for some answer to something.

"Wait a minute. Are you saying that someone used that phone call to report a murder over twenty miles away?"

"That's what I'm saying."

"Are you for real?"

"I'm not making this up Alice."

"I don't know if that camera pans down that far."

"Can we take a peek?"

Without saying a word, Alice makes her way around the counter and to the back of the store. I follow without invitation. We enter an unlocked door that leads into a small room that's no bigger than the closet of my old apartment. Well it's not old – just blown up. Stuffed in this cramped area are a desk, chair, and two filing cabinets. On the desk sits a newer computer system and on top of one of the cabinets sits a thirteen-inch monitor with a DVR system underneath.

"Alice, is this a digital system?"

"You bettcha. All I have to do is punch up the date on the computer so cross your fingers."

Alice takes a seat and boots up the system.

"Hey, do you think if my camera helps solve this case I would get a reward or something?"

"You know Alice, that's a great idea. If they don't give you one – I will."

With a smile on her face and a Marlboro between her lips, Alice hits the keyboard and in the blink of an eye, she pulls up the program. After the login and password, she looks over her right shoulder at me.

"Give me the date and time."

"October 1st – 11:54 in the morning."

Alice's pudgy fingers punch in the data with amazing precession. Instantly we see time as it was. Like a time machine, we're able to dial back and see what took place at this very spot, at that very time. As the camera lens picks up the images of that day, my fear is ever growing that the position of the unit is too high. That it's only going to catch the very top of the pole that secures the phone. I will know in a few seconds. I find it sweet that the same technology that framed me in the woods a month ago could possibly vindicate me as well.

The wait is excruciating as the eye of the camera reaches the tall menu sign at Taco Bell. The image is clear and my fingers and toes are crossed at this point. The camera then reaches the payphone and it is positioned a little high but if anyone is standing there, I'll be able to I.D. them. No one is standing at the phone, but as the camera continues to pan, a figure flashes across the screen.

"THERE HE IS!" I yell out. "Can you stop it?"

"No I can't. You're watching a recording. We'll have to wait until the cameras pans back the other way."

"But what if he's gone by then?"

"I guess no reward money for me – huh?"

I lean against the back wall. With my arms crossed and knees shaking, I attempt to keep my balance as we wait. We stare at the thirteen by thirteen inch screen like a pair of wannabe lottery winners waiting for that last number to appear.

"It looks like whoever just flashed on the screen was running to the phone. What do you think Alice?"

"I'd say. Did you recognize em?"

"No way – too fast."

"Well if we have to, I can go back and try to pause it. Maybe we'll get lucky."

Luck has nothing to do with this. The perpetrator is just stupid. Who wouldn't look around before making such a call to the police? I know I would. If it meant the difference between being a free man or a death row inmate, I'd be looking around. I would have cased the joint for weeks before taking such a chance. But then again, I wouldn't put myself into a situation like this. If criminals were smart, they wouldn't be criminals.

The anxiety builds as we watch the screen pan the front parking lot and starts its retreat back to where it began. The payphone soon appears again and Alice stops it perfectly to reveal an individual standing in all dark clothing, with the handset to their ear. The hood from their sweatshirt is loosely covering the back of the head, giving us a side view.

"Can you zoom in?"

Without hesitation, Alice centers the image and zooms in with amazing speed. The caller has a handkerchief over their mouth but the face is still visible. Instantly, my anxiety turns to anger. I see the person and cannot believe my eyes. I recognize the image. There is no doubt as to their identity. I clinch my fist in rage.

"You son-of-a-bitch you."

Alice looks up as I grab my cell and hit the desired speed-dial number.

"Do you know them?"

"You bet I do. How stupid can I be?"

I run from the store and my caller finally answers.

CHAPTER 36

"Sergeant Hanson"

"HANSON – WHERE ARE YOU?"

"I'm at the station Marvin – Why?"

"Where's Mandi. Is she working today?"

"No, it's her day off."

"IT'S HER MARK. DAMMIT IT'S HER. SHE'S THE ONE WHO CALLED IN THOSE DEATHS."

"Marvin, have you lost your mind?"

"If you don't believe me, go over to the Cigarette Depot and have the cashier show you the video."

"What video?"

"Mark, I don't have the time to explain to you what I've learned. But trust me on this one; she is somehow involved in the murders. I just watched a video of her making a call on the payphone at Taco Bell. The Depot has a surveillance camera set on at the corner of their building. We punched up the exact date and time of the first call. Mark, it was her."

"Are you sure?"

"Mark, I've slept with the woman. I think I know her from head to toe."

A silence drifts over my earpiece. I can imagine him staring into space trying to process all of this.

"Meet me over at her apartment Mark and bring your handcuffs. I don't have a set with me."

"Why don't you just call her?"

"NO! Don't call her. Just meet me at the apartment."

I smash the end bottom on my cell along with the gas pedal on my car. Her place is only five minutes away. I'm still fuming over what I saw. It doesn't make any sense. The thought that she was in some kind of trouble crosses my mind. Maybe someone was making her do all of this. But she would have said something. Every person I've ever met who works in the enforcement business has a little more backbone than your average Joe. Then again, if they threatened her family - Who knows.

I arrive at the apartment building and creep through the lot toward her place as if I was looking for a suspect. I guess at this point, I am. I'm calmer now than I was just a few minutes ago. The thought of Mandi being involved in this does not compute. We were a couple. She has to be in some kind of trouble. It's the only logical reason that makes any sense. Maybe the same goons who threatened me were threatening her the entire time. I hope that's it. I pity her if it's anything else.

I spot her apartment door and park well back. As I turn off the ignition, I catch movement to my right and see Hanson pulling in. He quickly parks and exits his vehicle.

"What the hell's going on Marvin?"

"I already told you what I know. What I don't know is why."

"Marvin, there's no way she made those calls. It was a man's voice on the other end."

"She had a handkerchief over her mouth. You even said the voice on the tape sounded muffled. Let's just go in here and talk to her, and I'll do the talking. I just need you to stand by."

"Okay, but I have no idea why I'm here."

"You're my backup."

"Should I shoot her if she runs?"

"No Mark, I'll take care of that."

"Great. I feel much better now."

We begin walking toward the only entrance to her place. A few bystanders are out gawking at us as we approach. I've become quite used to this part of the job. People always seem to have this burning need-to-know what is going on, even if it doesn't concern them. People like to watch other folks in trouble. It gives them the opportunity to sit back, play judge, and pat themselves on the back for living their lives better than them. Everyone has skeletons in their closet; just some are better at hiding them than others. Lord knows I've got my share.

"Do you see her car anywhere Marvin?"

"No I don't. Doesn't mean she's not home. They have underground parking here."

We arrive at the entrance and I take the lead. Several knocks on the front door fail to generate a response.

"Doesn't look like she's home" Hanson says.

I lean down and peak through the glass window with both hands shielding the light from the sides of my face. I see a furnished apartment with no signs that anyone is living here. No dishes in the sink; no knick-knacks on the coffee table; no anything that would give one any indication that this place is occupied.

"Mark, did she move?"

"Not that I'm aware."

"It looks as if she's gone. Here, take a look."

As Hanson assumes the same position, I secure my set of keys from my coat pocket and find the one Mandi gave me months ago.

"Mark, step aside."

He shuffles to his left without argument. I insert the key and we gain entry without incident. I head straight for the bedroom. If she's gone like we suspect, her closet will be the tail-tell sign. The bedroom door is open revealing no sheets on the bed. I look to my right and into an empty bedroom closet.

"Hanson, come here and look."

"Where the hell did she go, Marvin?"

"What did I tell you?"

"She's scheduled to work tonight too."

"You may want to call someone in to cover."

"I hear ya."

"Marvin, I'm going to head over to the cigarette place. Are you coming?"

"No, I need to make a stop first. You go ahead. Alice is the cashier and she'll show you the video."

"I'm not calling this in yet. I want you to know that. We don't really have any hard evidence on her."

"Yeah, but you got to admit; something's fishy here."

"I agree with you. Your hunches are better than most people's facts."

"I'll take that as a compliment."

"You should. Meet me back at the station when you're done. I'd ask where you're going but you wouldn't tell me anyway, so why waste my time."

"You're getting to know me quite well."

"You know you still owe me an explanation about your dad – Remember?"

"You help me with this and you got it."

"Watch your back Marvin."

"That's all I've been doing lately."

CHAPTER 37

I ease back the long driveway to the cabin. I still have the lock in my pocket for the freezer. I've been so preoccupied with everything going on, I forgot about locking dad up. I cannot imagine anyone finding this place up here. Dad was smart when he picked this location to stay out of sight. The entrance is right at a curve in the road. You'd have to be looking for this place to find it.

I pull up to the cabin and turn off the engine. A quick scan of the area finds nothing out of place. Everything is right where I left it the other day. I exit my vehicle and walk toward the front door, making sure each step is deliberately placed on the circular concrete steps dad had laid down. Old habits die hard you know. Don't want to track any mud inside. Like anyone would care.

The front door is unlocked and I enter the residence knowing that. I make my way through the cold living room and into the kitchen. As I arrive adjacent to the kitchen table, I see something now that doesn't belong. A white van is parked up tight against the back of the cabin, out of view from the front of the property. I take a few steps toward the kitchen window to take a closer look. My heart is racing with the thought that someone is here. If they are, it's too late for me to do anything but run. But even that option may not be available to me. I sense a presence behind me and don't even get the chance to turn around before I hear the sound of metal clicking - the sound of a gun being manually placed in the firing position.

"Don't move, Riggs or I'll kill you right now."

I do as I'm told. The female voice behind me has a desperate tone about her. One must know when to fight and when to back off in order to live sometimes.

"Hello Mandi. I've been looking for you."

"I'll bet you have."

"You better kill me now bitch, because if I get the chance, I'm taking your ass out."

"I don't think so, Riggs. You'd have to kill both of us and I don't think you're that fast anymore."

My peripheral vision catches sight of another figure standing to my left. I roll my eyes over and see the second half of the gangster duo leaning against the freezer holding a gun as well."

"So Mandi, mind filling me in on what the HELL is going on?"

"Just a little payback."

"What payback?"

"Where's your father?"

"What do you care?"

She steps forward and presses the gun into the back my skull.

"I said where is he?"

"Screw you bitch. I'm not telling you anything until I get some answers."

"DON'T CALL ME BITCH AGAIN OR I SWEAR, I'll..."

"You won't do anything. First of all, I don't think you have the guts and secondly, you need me for something. I'm not sure for what though."

"Don't under estimate me asshole. I'm here for one reason and one reason only: To bury your old man, just like he buried mine."

In less time than it takes to flick on a light switch, I have the answers to my question: The reason for my world being turned up side down. And the one person who I thought I could trust is the very same person who doesn't care whether I'm alive or dead."

"So you're Kass's daughter."

"Where's your father Riggs, and I'm not going to ask too many more times."

"Mandi, he had nothing to do with your father being murdered in the shop."

"The hell he didn't. He just left him there. He did everything he could to cover it up so he could save his own hide.

"Mandi, he did it to save mine. He knew that whoever killed your old man would be coming after me eventually."

"Bullshit! He did it for himself. He even stole my dad's motor home in the process."

"So this is all about revenge?"

"This is about righting a wrong. My father is buried in a grave marked with a tombstone that does not bear his name. Like he was a nobody; like he never existed. My father was a good man. He deserves better."

"I guess you feel somewhat guilty seeing that you caused all of this."

"What do you mean by that?"

"What I mean is you're the one who was banging Winger behind Daddy's back. If you would have stuck with your own age group, there wouldn't have been a fight and your old man wouldn't have taken a shot to his head with that lead pipe."

"How do you know about that?"

"No comment."

Mandi is getting more enraged as we talk. I can tell by the increase in pressure on the back of my head she is applying with her 9mm. I'm pissed myself. Pissed that all this crap is happening to me. Pissed that I was so gullible that I left my defenses down and allowed this woman into my life. I should have known this relationship was just coming along too easily. They never go that smoothly in my world.

But if I'm going to survive this one, I need to come up with something quick. What if I told them where dad was? Maybe seeing him dead will put this drama to an end. What do I have to lose.

"Okay Mandi. I'll tell you where my dad is but you have to promise to let me go after I do."

Mandi pauses for a few seconds.

"Deal – Where is he?"

"He's right behind your friend."

"There's nothing there but a freezer."

"Open it."

Mandi signals to her hired hand to do just that. I hear creaking from the rusty hinges as the lid on the freezer is lifted. I also hear a gasp from my guests as they cannot believe their eyes.

"He's dead."

"I told you he was."

"But how? I wanted to do it. I wanted to be the one."

"Sorry, girl. I found him dead in his easy chair a few weeks ago right out here on his back patio. It was either a heart attack or a stroke. Not sure which."

"Dammit. Then I'll just kill you instead."

"Mandi! I did nothing wrong here."

"Yes you did. You allowed him to keep his secret. You did everything within your power to make sure he lived.

"You're right, I did. You would have done the same."

"No I wouldn't have. I'd a stood up and took my lumps."

"Oh bullshit. You and I both know better."

"You think you know me. Our relationship was an act; don't

forget that. I played you. I played you just to get information. But you wouldn't budge. You were so committed to keeping the secret, you would have given your own life to keep it.

"That's right."

"So finally I decided if I couldn't get what I wanted, I'd make sure they would put you away."

"So you killed those hunters?"

"No I didn't, but I set it up. Did you like the touch with the digital camera and your hunting suit?"

"But it didn't work – did it?"

"You and your damn GPS system. If it weren't for that, they would have locked you up and the key melted down. But that's okay. I'll get my revenge. And I know just how you can repay your debt to me."

"I owe you nothing Mandi."

The next thing I remember is the pressure of metal on the back of my head releasing, followed by constellations of stars circling me after the impact. I had no idea I was knocked unconscious until about an hour later.

CHAPTER 38

I awake from a sound sleep with a splitting headache. It's the kind that reaches all the way to the back of one's neck. But mine started there. It's what usually happens when your ex-girlfriend nails you in the back of your head with a handgun.

One would normally rub the area where the pain is generating in hopes of relieve it, but that won't happen in this case. I'm handcuffed. As I squirm to get myself free, I find she's done a masterful job: Even took the time to lock each one.

With a few squints, I begin to regain my focus and discover that I'm lying in the back of a moving cargo van. I can only assume it's the same one I saw hidden behind the cabin.

As the seconds roll by and my vision improves in the dimly lit vehicle, I lift my head in an attempt to get a better look at what I'm dealing with. I see Mandi in the passenger's seat and I assume her sidekick is driving. Neither are talking nor paying me any attention right now. Both are just looking ahead and appear to be searching for something. I also begin to feel a presence lying beside me. The presence is cold – real cold. Whatever it is is wrapped in a sheet and if it weren't for these damn cuffs, I'd investigate further.

I manage to lift my upper body so now I'm in a much more comfortable sitting position. The left side of my body is numb from lying on the van's floor. I can only imagine how long I've been lying here. I can't reach my cell but I know it has to be after five o'clock: Daylight savings time and all.

"Good evening sleepy-head" I hear from the front of the van.

"I Swear to God Mandi, you've signed your death warrant with this one

"Screw you, Riggs, and your tough talk. I'm getting sick of hearing it. You are in no position to threaten anyone."

"I'll shut up when you kill me. Mind telling me where we're at?"

"Not at all. We're just pulling into the cemetery now."

"What cemetery?"

"The one where my father is buried."

I look out the front windshield and can see she's not making this up. We've been on the road for a good hour while I lay there unconscious. I catch a glimpse of the sign for the Greencastle Cemetery - a place where many of my relatives have been laid to rest. Both of my grandparents are here, my cousin April, and a number of acquaintances that have graced my presence over the years. They're all here. And if I don't get out of these cuffs soon and stop this nonsense, I'll be joining the reunion way before my time.

"Did you enjoy your time with your dad?" Mandi says while still holding the gun on me.

"What do you mean by that?"

"What I mean is you and your old man have been lying together back there for an hour. Did you have a chance to get caught up on things?"

I look beside me with better vision now and can see the outline of a man under the white sheet. Mandi reaches back and yanks the sheet toward her, revealing the frozen body of my father."

"What is this, Mandi? What's churning in that pea-brain of yours?"

"You'll see soon enough."

The van comes to a stop while she finishes her chuckling. Like a mad woman who has lost touch of all reality, she exits her side of the van and continues the comic routine in her head until both rear doors swings open.

"Get out" she demands

"Fuck you!"

"I SAID GET OUT!"

"No."

Her male accomplice lunges at me and attempts to grab my shirt. With one quick kick, I nail him square in the face, sending him flying backwards onto the ground. He is a large man who I suspect won't stay down long. I need to be ready to fight when he collects himself. My wait is not long.

Within seconds he's at me again. But this time he jumps into the van and pins my legs against the floor. He grabs the collar of my shirt and pulls my face into his. With his right hand, he chambers a round into his automatic and presses the barrel into my temple.

"AMOS, NO! Not yet."

Amos says nothing. Like a dog that's been told to heel, he obeys without saying a word."

"Come on, Amos – do it. You'd better take your shot now cause you might not get another one."

"AMOS, get him out of the van." Mandi exclaims.

With a sudden jerk of his twenty-inch biceps, Amos launches me out of the van by my collar and I land helplessly onto the cold, wet ground. I was lucky though: My face caught my fall.

Before I can gain my composure, I feel Mandi behind me unlocking and removing my newly acquired jewelry.

"Get up" she demands.

"Why."

"Because you have work to do."

"I don't think so."

From the back of the van, I watch as Amos retrieves a shovel and pickaxe. He throws both items in my direct, which land inches from my face.

"Start digging, Riggs."

Her words made no sense until she was kind enough to shine the flashlight on a headstone in front of me. It was the marker of my father's grave.

"You're going to right this wrong tonight, Riggs, or I'll kill you right now."

"You want me to dig up your father. Are you kidding me?"

"You've got over eight hours of darkness to get it down. The ground's not frozen down here yet. There's plenty of time to put the right person where he belongs."

I can't believe what's happening here. She's lost it. She wants her father so badly; she'll take his dead corpse just to have him. That's why they brought dad along. Now I have to make a decision to either fight or cooperate. I don't want to do either but that option is not available. My decision is quickly made. I will dig. I will make sure I take the full eight plus hours. And while digging, I can come up with a plan. Or maybe they'll both get tired and fall asleep. I have more options digging. I reach over and secure the pickaxe. The dig begins . . .

CHAPTER 39

Not quite sure how long I've been at this but my back could probably tell you. I've tried to take my time but my captors are sitting in the back of the van with the doors wide open, refusing to answer any of my questions. All I've heard for the last few hours are the words dig and die. I can tell you one thing; when this is all over, they won't take me out without a fight.

I've had plenty of time to come up with a plan of action but nothing that really tickles my fancy. The best plan that has come to mind is jumping out of this hole and sticking one of them with this pickaxe. Problem is I wouldn't be able to get both of them. One or the other would shoot me dead before I could get another swing. But at least I'd get Mandi. That's all I want right now – revenge.

I stand briefly as I've done a few times since being forced into this situation, in order to stretch out my back muscles. A man in his forties should not be digging holes. I could see if I was putting in a mailbox post or digging up some petunias at the house: but a grave?

The air is cold this evening but my body is warm. I haven't worked this hard since being employed as a tree surgeon back in Florida. I was fresh out of the Army and in the best shape of my life. My mom hooked me up with Ken who ran his own tree business. His wife and my mom were friends at the time. I almost didn't make it through the first week. Spending all day throwing one hundred pound logs into the back of a dump truck would kick anyone's ass. But it was a job, and forty bucks-a-day cash wasn't bad either, back then.

I can hear the chilly breeze blowing above me as the walls from this grave shelter my body. I'm close. I'm real close to striking gold. I know because on this particular break, I can no longer see the outline of headstones that cover this hillside. All I can see now is the top layer of soil that I have dug with my own two hands. I quickly conclude that since I'm six-feet tall and most graves are six feet deep, my time on this earth maybe short. I should be hitting a casket any minute now.

Two more swings of my pickaxe ends with a "thud."

"What was that?" I hear Mandi holler. Instantly, she arrives at the edge of the pit and looks down at me.

"What was that?" she says again.

"Well since I'm digging up a grave, I would wager that it's your old man. So now what?"

"You need to get the coffin open and bring my dad up here."

"You're kidding?"

"Do I look like I'm kidding?"

"So this is your plan, huh? You want to switch the bodies?"

"No, you are. My father will have a proper burial."

"And if I refuse…"

"Then I'll kill you right now and have Amos pull him out."

"I guess I really don't have a choice, do I?"

"It's your choice, Riggs. Either die now or ten minutes from now."

"I'm going to get you bitch. I don't know how but I'm going to get you."

Mandi just smiles and walks out of my line of sight. I'm starting to get scared now. I revert back to my pickaxe idea and decide that it's my best chance. I probably won't survive but I'm not going out like some coward. If I go – she goes.

I brush off two years of dirt from the coffin that lies before my feet. I now have both latches exposed, and the moment I've dreaded is now upon me. I have to make a move. I can't wait any longer. The time for stalling is finished.

I stare at the coffin that we put in the ground two years earlier. Its beauty has diminished but the sadness of that day is still with me. If I had known this man was not my father, I would have never told the funeral director to bury him with his hunting cap and rifle.

RIFLE – OH MY GOD!!!

"Come on Riggs – today!" I hear Mandi say from above me.

"Be done soon sweetheart."

I immediately hit the first latch with the pickaxe and break it on the first try.

"What are you doing down there Riggs?"

"I'm breaking off the latches. You do know they seal these things before they go in the ground?"

I hear footsteps coming my way.

"Mandi, you may not want to see this."

"Why?"

"You do know the people who killed your father, blew his head off – right?"

A moment of silence echoes through the cemetery.

"Just hurry up."

I hit the other latch with the same precision, and the seal is broken. I throw the pick-axe to the side and reach down to open the lid, praying to God that the funeral home honored my wishes and put the rifle in here as I had instructed them to do.

I manage to get my fingers under a small lip and thrust the lid open. The smell is bad, but not as bad as I had anticipated. With the small amount of light available thanks to a full moon, I witness a skeleton wearing a three-piece suit holding the rifle I had prayed for. I secure the rusty piece of hardware and flip it over to check for a clip.

YES!!!

With the quickness of a gazelle leaping in the air to avoid the hungry lion, I catapult from the grave and scope my target from only a few feet away. Both are staring at me with their jaws in the open and locked position.

"Weren't expecting this, were ya bitch?"

I get no response from the once dynamic duo.

"Both of you drop your guns now."

Without hesitation they comply.

"Amos, lie flat on your stomach and I would strongly suggest you not make any sudden moves. And you, Ms. Kass - you can get on your knees."

"I won't do it."

"Oh yes you will."

I take a step toward her. Keeping one eye on Amos as he makes his way down to the ground, I quickly thrust the stock of the rifle at her head, making contact and watch as she hits the ground. Standing over her, I place the end of the rifle against the back of her head.

"How's it feel sweetheart? You like that cold steel feeling?"

"Where the hell did you get that rifle?"

"Well if you would have attended the funeral you would have known that I buried him with his hunting rifle. But you weren't there. I guess banging Winger was more important."

"Marvin, please don't kill me."

"Oh, so now it's Marvin. When you had the upper hand it was Riggs. Funny how that works."

"Please, I beg you – don't kill me. I'll do anything."

"Yeah, I've heard that before. I'll make a deal with you babe. You start talking and I'll consider taking your ass out quick."

I get no response.

"Who is Amos?"

"He's a guy I hired."

"To do what?"

"To help me frame you."

"Well that's obvious. I want to know why Mandi. What made you think that me rotting in prison would help you?"

"I already told you back at the cabin, I couldn't find your dad anywhere. And if I couldn't get him, I'd at least get you."

"So this is all about payback."

"Damn right it is. But every stink'n time I thought you were out of the picture...that damn GPS system in your vehicle. I never thought of it."

"Who killed those hunters, Mandi? Was it you?"

"No, it was Amos' brother."

Amos turns his head and looks up at me.

"I'll bet you haven't seen your brother lately?"

Amos just stares.

"Just so you know, he won't be coming around anytime soon. He's kind of at the bottom of a quarry."

"You killed his brother."

"I ask the questions here. So it was you who took my hunting suit from the closet?"

"Yeap!"

"And why was Winger in my apartment?"

"He was snooping around trying to find something on your dad's whereabouts. But the dumb shit goes in there and doesn't tell anyone. Amos' brother was waiting outside and saw a figure walking around through the window. He assumed it was you and hit the switch.

"So you called me on my cell that day to make sure I was dead

– not alive. You piece of shit! I bet you almost dropped the phone when I answered – didn't ya? But you missed me. Instead you kill your boyfriend. You really suck at this Mandi; I mean bad."

"Whatever" she replies in defeat.

Her lack of concern enrages me. For the last few months everything she's said has been a lie. Everything she pretended was to be an elaborate scheme to see my undoing. With the barrel of the rifle still against her head, I jack a round into the chamber so she can feel what it's like to have no control over her fate. I click the safety off and return the butt of the gun to my shoulder. I see Amos turn his head away. He doesn't want to be a witness to what I'm about to do. That's probably not a bad idea. Doesn't really matter though. He'll be next. With my finger on the trigger and my target sobbing, I attempt to talk myself out of this, but I can't. Why should she live?

"FREEZE MARVIN" I hear from behind me.

"Hanson?"

"Put the gun down Marvin."

I turn my head and see him standing a few feet away among a group of other officers, all with guns pointed at me.

"Do what he says Bro" another voice echoes from the crowd.

I then see Adam walk to the front. He's the only one not armed.

"Marvin, we heard everything. You don't have to kill her."

"Adam, what are you doing here? How did you know I was here?"

Before I can get an answer, Hanson approaches and grabs a hold of the rifle to keep me from pulling the trigger. I release without putting up any resistance. I see a sigh of relief come over his face.

"Your brother called me when he arrived at the cabin and found your father's body missing from the freezer."

"Yeah bro, along with the blood on the floor and the tire tracks dug into the back yard of the cabin, I knew you were in trouble."

"But how did you find me."

"Your cell phone of course."

"What do you mean?"

"Remember that locator feature I gave you hell about not having on and I made you turn on? I work for a cell phone company dude. I can find anyone."

With a sigh of relief myself, I drop the rifle. Officers converge on the pair and handcuff both without delay. As two of the officers get Mandi to her feet, she looks at me with a revengeful glare. It was a look that I will not forget: A look that tells me that until my dying day, there will be a soul in this world who will hate the mere fact that I exist. I will forever have to look over my shoulder. Adam puts his hand on my shoulder.

"So, Marvin, who's the chick."

"Hanson didn't tell you?"

"No. We drove up here in separate cars. Remember, I was the one with the tracking equipment."

"Oh Yeah. Well that "chick" as you so eloquently put it was my girlfriend."

"Really?

"Yeah"

"Got some news for you Marvin?"

"What's that?"

"You're going to need a new one."

"Very funny.

CHAPTER 40

It's sunny out today and not a cloud anywhere. I've often wondered how it is the sun can shine so brightly in the sky and it still be twenty degrees outside. Maybe the sun isn't as powerful as they say it is. Or maybe it's so far away that it has no bearing on the weather here. Either way, it's a beautiful morning in the mountains.

I've made the rocky cliffs my home today, as I've done so many times throughout my life. I lean back and thank the Powers-that-be for allowing me to stay on this earth. No man should be given as many chances at life as I've had over the last few years. I'd like to think my actions and bravery had something to do with it. But how do you explain the rifle in the coffin? Just luck or spiritual intervention?

It's the first day of gun season here in Pennsylvania. For a game warden that means no one has a day off today, nor for the rest of the week for that matter. I had to quit my job and agree not to discuss any aspects of what took place to avoid prosecution. It was kind of a no-brainer if you ask me. If I didn't agree, then I would go to jail and lose my job anyway.

Mandi and her hired hand have both been charged with murder

and conspiracy to commit. It's been the top story for most of the last week on the news. Come to find out, it was Amos' brother who killed those three hunters. Mandi paid each of them ten thousand dollars for the job. Innocent lives snuffed out because of me, because I just had to keep a secret. I guess when all is said and done there are no secrets in life. All will eventually come to life.

With no job or place to live, I've had to make some life decisions that no one my age should have to ponder. I do have options. I could go to Florida and stay with mom, or head back to Wisconsin and hopefully get my old bank job back. But my time here in this world is growing ever shorter by the minute, and who wouldn't want to visit heaven before they actually get there.

I've fixed up the cabin and have made it a pretty comfortable home for myself. I got a job down at the grocery store and start this Saturday. Seven-fifty an hour doesn't sound like much, but when you live up here, you don't need six figures to maintain a life.

I catch sight of a twig moving in the narrow ravine below. I take another look and to my surprise, a deer appears from behind an old tree trunk. I ready my sights. The deer is about thirty-five yards away. Then another deer appears – and another – and still another. It was the fifth one that caught my attention. A nice eight-point buck, and he has not yet detected my presence. I raise my weapon and with one eye peer through the scope, making sure to get him centered just right. I push the safety off and ease down on the trigger.

"CLICK"

The camera shutter captures a moment in time to be enjoyed for years to come. No more killing...

Michael Koontz is a 1980 graduate from the Greencastle Antrim High School in Greencastle, Pennsylvania. He began writing of his experiences as a MP in the US Army and a Police Officer in the State of Florida, which progressed into a passion for writing fictional stories. He brings a down-to-earth style of writing to his audience making for an easy, comfortable reading experience. He currently resides in Waukesha, Wisconsin where he continues to write and raise his two daughters.